Enj!

LAROCHE

Hunter

Manhver Island

2020

:)

Murder on the
SCONSET EXPRESS

Hunter Laroche

authorHOUSE®

AuthorHouse™
1663 Liberty Drive
Bloomington, IN 47403
www.authorhouse.com
Phone: 1 (800) 839-8640

Published by AuthorHouse   07/01/2015

ISBN: 978-1-5049-1878-7 (sc)
ISBN: 978-1-5049-1879-4 (e)

Library of Congress Control Number: 2015910137

Print information available on the last page.

Any people depicted in stock imagery provided by Thinkstock are models, and such images are being used for illustrative purposes only. Certain stock imagery © Thinkstock.

This book is printed on acid-free paper.

A Nantucket murder mystery that takes place in the
early 1940's
(Yes the author knows the train had stopped running prior
to that time!)

When a couple arrives on this picturesque quaint
island, their lives are mesmerized by its beauty, until
a murder takes place dragging them
into the turn of events...

Coming soon "The Wauwinet Caper" penned by Hunter Laroche

This book is dedicated in memory of John Krebs

John was the first person I met upon my arrival on Nantucket in 1979. An old Caribbean smuggler had referred me to the Ships Inn and instructed me to ask for John. Who knew that our friendship would take us to many Buffett concerts and down to the shores of Culebra Island, where Mary, John, and I would enjoy watercress sandwiches on the beach, beautiful sunsets, and good times. This book is for you, my dear friend.

Hunter Laroche

I would like to thank Marshall DuBock for his time and patience in our many conversations regarding this story. To Simon Gilmore (author of *The Adventures of Mr Hawkins*) from Dartmouth, England, for his guidance, knowledge, and thoughts. To John Shea, my friend and mentor. Let's not forget Jeffrey Cook (Lights, Camera, Action, Cooker), actor and playwright with whom I can't ever hold a conversation where tears don't flow from my eyes from the laughter that ensues. And most importantly, to my wife, Karen. Without her numerous hours of reading and reworking and reworking, you would not be holding this book that hopefully you are going to enjoy reading. XOXO

Murder on the Sconset Express

Nantucket Island settled in 1659 "for the sum of thirty pounds ... and also two beaver hats, one for me and one for my wife." As a whaling town, it was actually commented on in Chapter 14 of *Moby-Dick*: "The very heart and soul of Nantucket is the original whaler and fishermen and those who loved them." Now it is one of the wealthiest summer residences in the United States. In 1940, it was something grittier. It was all heart and solitude and the wide-open whale of a sea.

CHAPTER ONE

It was late in the evening at Cy's Green Coffee Pot Restaurant and Bar on Nantucket. The tavern clock's gold numbers glowed against its black finish.

KW had swiped the bar one last time with his rag and then polished a few beer steins before climbing the rickety wooden ladder to clean and wind the old London-style clock. He thought to himself, *How many times has that pendulum swung back and forth? I wonder who the original owner of the old clock was.* That was a recurring thought that swept through his head almost every time he hand-wound the clock. KW often thought that he should send a letter, along with a photograph of the clock, to the company whose brass plate was on the bottom inside door of the unit.

*Schessling and Sons Fine Clock Makers
Dresden, Germany, founded in 1829*

KW thought they might find it interesting to see how it was holding up and the fact that it was on a small island thirty miles out to sea in another country.

Almost every evening after the last smattering of patrons had cleared out, it was the same ritual: KW checked to make sure the front, back, and kitchen doors were secured shut. Then he would go get a broom and sweep around the bar area before he pulled out the stepladder to tend to the clock.

Earlier this evening he had thought to himself, *With this front blowing through, it's gonna be a quiet night for business.* Only a smattering of people came in after the movie at the Dreamland Theater. *The Philadelphia Story* was advertised as coming soon, as well as *The Fighting 69th*, with James Cagney. KW was going to try to get free time to see both of those.

It was around nine thirty. KW was going to close up, as the last customers had just departed, when the front door opened and a man walked in all wet, his glasses foggy. He had no hat on, and he asked KW if the tavern was still open. He remembered what Tracy Root, the maître d' of the Chanticleer Inn, always told him: "KW, first impressions are lasting ones in the restaurant and hospitality business. Don't ever judge a book by its cover. What you discover also might surprise you."

KW replied, "I was getting ready to close up, but sure, come on in. Grab a seat at the bar. I'll be glad to get you a drink. I might just start cleaning up a little while you're here. Not the best weather out there tonight."

"You've got that right," the man replied. He added, "My name's Richard. Just arrived a short time ago on the boat. Kinda rough seas out there."

"I bet so. Wind's been kicking up pretty good since early afternoon. Rain's been coming down sideways most of the day," replied KW. "Where are you staying?"

"I have a house on Broad Street. Purchased it last year and have had a crew working on it for the past ten months or so."

"You have that really nice Victorian next to Dolly and Nobby's, the Nesbit Inn?"

"That's the one!"

"Well, it's really nice. I was lucky enough to take a tour of the inside a few weeks back."

"You did?" Richard asked.

"Yeah. A friend of mine, David Crosier, is your painting contractor. I met him various times while on the island also, right here, prior to purchasing the bar. So when he heard I was going to be the new proprietor, one of his first questions he had was 'Are you going to keep Sylvia on in the kitchen?' I told him that was the plan. David said, 'Wow, that's a relief. She's the best cook around!'

"He does an excellent job. He's very meticulous with every detail, from paint to wallpaper and everything else you throw at him. David did some work for me here right before I opened. I traded his labor for food and beverage credit. He loved that idea. I had a question for him on some shelving that I was considering adding in the kitchen, so I wandered over to your house, as I knew he was still working on it. He took me for a quick walk-through. You've done an excellent job restoring that."

"Well, we are almost finished. I just thought I would come and see the progress. I haven't been back since I purchased it, and I am really pleased with the way it has turned out."

"Where do you hail from, Richard?"

"Chicago. I am in the banking business. My wife, Inese, arrives tomorrow with her mother, Anita. They're coming in from Europe. I hope the weather clears somewhat."

"What can I get you to drink?" asked KW.

"Do you have a nice red wine?"

"Well, all I pour is Inglenook Cabernet by the glass."

"Do you have anything better?" Richard inquired.

"Well, by the bottle, I have two French and two Spanish and one Italian and two from California."

3

"What are the French?"

"I have, let's see, a Chateau Greysac 1938 and a Chateau Gloria 1936."

"I'll take the Gloria. If I don't finish it, can you cork it and leave for me for tomorrow?"

"Sure, no problem," KW replied.

As KW set one of his few wineglasses in front of him, Richard looked up and asked, "Do you have any better glasses?"

"No, sorry, this is all I have to offer."

"Well, I tell ya, KW, this seems like a nice tavern, but we've got to work on your wine selection and your stemware!"

"We don't get much call for fancy wines here. Mostly just one or two of our customers ask for better wines, like Pirate Pete, Duff Myercord, and Neil Krauter. The rest is beer and whiskey."

"So you do get a few requests for some better wines?"

"Yes," replied KW. "Duff Myercord enjoys a nice wine that he calls heavy. Pirate Pete likes a French Bordeaux, and Neil Krauter—well, he comes in and just says give me the best you got!" KW said while chuckling.

"That sounds like my type of guy," Richard replied. "What does this guy Neil do? He lives here?" Richard asked very curiously.

"Well, he is here often, even in the wintertime. He lives in New York and Boston and also has places in Paris and Portugal. I met him a couple of years ago. He owns insurance companies in New York, Boston, Dallas, San Francisco, and Washington, DC. The list of his companies seems to go on and on. He actually insures my little place here in trade for food, but he is adamant about paying for his alcohol or wines, and he enjoys a lot of wine! He is something else, that Neil." KW broke out into a good laugh.

Richard joined KW in a loud laugh. "He sounds like a great guy to me. I'd love to meet him."

"Well, you never know around here when he will pop in, with a pretty broad on his arm, of course," KW added, still smiling.

At that point Richard pulled out from his carrying case several folded newspapers and magazines, which he promptly placed on the bar. "Can I get anything to eat?"

Again, KW remembered the words of his friend Tracy, who stopped in almost every Wednesday. KW said, "I don't have much, as the kitchen closed at 8:00 p.m., but let me see what I can whip up. Do you like chicken? We had a nice special tonight: Sylvia's Italian herb-roasted chicken served with green beans and buttermilk mashed potatoes."

"That sounds perfect," Richard replied.

After KW got Richard all set up with his wine, he retreated into the kitchen to make him a plate of chicken. Within fifteen minutes a piping hot dish with a quarter of a roasted chicken, mashed potatoes, green beans, and gravy arrived, which KW placed in front of Richard. Richard was grinning from ear to ear and dug right in. He never took his eyes off the newspaper. Finally, he glanced up and said, "Let me tell you, that was one excellent dish. So simple but the flavors were excellent." When he had finished and KW was clearing his plate, Richard asked, "Dessert?"

KW replied, "Only Sylvia's warm homemade blueberry pie à la mode with hand-churned vanilla bean ice cream."

Richard looked like a kid in a candy store when it arrived. Then he asked, "Coffee?"

KW corked up the rest of the wine, put it on what he referred to as his private shelf, brought Richard his coffee, and went about finishing his chores. He glanced over every now and again to see that Richard was still engulfed in his newspapers. KW had nowhere to go, so he let Richard take his time. KW sat down a few bar stools away. Richard put down his newspaper and started asking about the business, how long he had been working there, and, if he owned it, how the lease and profit margin were.

Right then Marshmallow, the house cat, hopped up onto the bar, walked right over to the newspapers, and sat on them. She let out a big meow, happy and content.

"Oh, by the way, that's Marshmallow," KW said with a chuckle.

Richard smiled and said, "Well, I better let you close up. You wouldn't happen to have a glass of port, would you?"

"One of my favorite nightly rituals is to end with a glass of Fonseca tawny port," KW replied. Grabbing two glasses, he poured them both two fingers. "That's on me," KW told Richard. "Welcome to Cy's."

Marshmallow let out another meow, and they both started laughing. Richard asked for the tab, and he pulled some money out of his wallet, not really counting it, and placed it on the bar. When KW picked it up, Richard was already getting off the bar stool.

KW said, "Wait a minute, Richard. There's way too much money here!"

Richard looked at him and said, "That's fine. Grab a drink on your next day off."

"But, Richard …" KW started to reply when Richard just walked out the door. KW breathed out a sigh of exhaustion as he walked behind Richard to lock the door. He talked and hummed to himself. "Not bad for a stormy night."

Marshmallow purred loudly and rubbed against an empty whiskey bottle.

"Gonna take a long, easy sleep tonight, kitty cat?" He glanced over at Marshmallow and realized what great company she turned out to be.

Sylvia's Blueberry Pie
    1 ½ tbs lemon juice
    4 cups native blueberries
    1/3 cup flour
    1 cup sugar
    2 tsp butter
    1/4 tsp cinnamon

Combine flour, sugar, and cinnamon. Add blueberries. Place in pastry shell. Sprinkle lemon juice. Dot the top of the blueberry mix with pats of butter. Add top crust, and pierce a few holes in top pastry. Bake at 425°F for 45–50 minutes.

CHAPTER TWO

KW had only purchased the bar a week earlier when he placed a sign on the front door window: CLOSED FOR REMODELING. He thought with a few changes to the menu, beer, and liquor offerings, he would be back open within seven to ten days. A little touch-up to the old wooden floors, a fresh coat of paint, a few new paintings, and a little spiff-up here and there would be a nice touch—nothing dramatic, as he knew the saying, "If it ain't broke don't fix it!"

Cy's Green Coffee Pot had been an institution for years, with a steady clientele. People loved their food, which was due to Ms. Sylvia's cooking. It was a great location in the heart of town close to the ferry pier and fishing boats. The tavern had a rustic, warm atmosphere.

KW had been a patron many times over the years since he had been visiting the island. He was enjoying lunch at Les's Lunch Counter in Mignosa's Market when he overheard the person next to him tell Les that old Rob and Connie Slimmon might be selling Cy's. KW then caught most of the conversation about how the couple were thinking of retiring and moving to a warmer climate.

KW stopped in Cy's and chatted with Rob Slimmon the next day. Rob had met KW on several occasions prior. They had a nice, detailed conversation in one of the back booths. After a while they agreed that the tavern would be leased to KW with the option of purchasing the building.

After KW took over the ownership, he was cleaning up outside when he noticed a kitten sitting in the bushes, staring at him while he swept the sidewalk. He gave out a "Hello, kitty! How are you today?" The cat just sat and stared at KW for a while. KW went about his business. A memory flashed in his head. He thought of the first time he saw the kitten a few days earlier. She was a tiny little thing with black and white fur. She was chasing a leaf around in the sunlight on the grass across the street one afternoon in the park by the Atheneum.

Sylvia, who had been asked by KW to remain and run the kitchen for the restaurant, had agreed after they discussed it over coffee and muffins. KW told her he would like to revise the menu, keeping her favorites and adding some new dishes. Sylvia loved the idea, as the Slimmons were not much for change. "Just leave it be," Rob would say to Sylvia. She would just smile and nod at his opinion. Mr. Slimmon would often say to Sylvia, "Customers are enjoying what we offer."

A few days later, as they were nearing the opening deadline, Sylvia was making a batch of s'mores for KW to sample. Sylvia thought they might like to offer them as a dessert once in a while. Right when she was almost done, she looked up to see the cutest black-and-white kitten staring inside from the ledge near the kitchen window. She said, "Oh my! What a beautiful kitten you are!" Right at that moment, the kitten put her paw on the window, almost like a wave. Sylvia opened up the kitchen door, and the kitten strolled right in and let out a meow.

Sylvia got a saucer from the cabinet and poured some milk into it. The kitten lapped it right up and started purring away. Then the kitten jumped up to a corner shelf and proceeded to stick her head inside a bag of marshmallows.

KW walked into the kitchen, being drawn in by the aroma of the baking s'mores, and saw the kitten with her head inside the marshmallow bag and let out a laugh. Sylvia told him about seeing her outside the window and how the cat almost waved to her through the glass. He told Sylvia how he had seen the cat a few times across the street in the park. They both laughed, as now the kitten had managed to get totally inside the almost-empty bag of marshmallows. Then almost simultaneously they said, "Who do you think she belongs to?" They agreed that she looked kind of skinny to have a home to go to.

Sylvia then pulled the kitten out of the paper bag, gave her a kiss, and said, "All right, you little marshmallow, time to go. I have a kitchen to run, and it's not meant for kitties!" She placed the kitten back outside and shut the door. But the cat did not leave. She hopped right back up on the window ledge and kept staring in at Sylvia.

KW loved the s'mores and thought they would make a great fit, thinking they should offer a set dessert on set days. Again, in the kitchen, he saw the kitten staring at him through the window, and he said, "Hello, Marshmallow. Nowhere to go?"

Late that evening when KW was closing up, he went into the kitchen. Out on the ledge was the kitten again, so he opened up the door, let her back inside, and put out a little dish of tuna fish that Sylvia had made for sandwiches earlier in the day. He figured there was no harm in letting the cat stay inside if she felt so inclined.

He hustled the kitten out into the bar area after her snack, and she seemed to feel right at home. She found a booth that seemed to be made for her, hopped up on it, curled right up, and dozed off. When he was just about to lock up for the night, KW picked up the cat, placed her outside, and said, "Okay, home you go, little Marshmallow." But instead of trailing off, she just stared at KW, as if she had nowhere to go. He thought to himself, *She is too young to stay outside alone at night.* In one swoop, he picked up the kitten and said, "Okay, you little Marshmallow, you're coming home with me!"

Sylvia and KW both asked around to see if they could locate little Marshmallow's proper owners, but no one seemed to know. Sylvia asked the group from the ladies' club and also posted a note on the public board on Main Street but to no avail. Next thing you know, Marshmallow became the house cat of the pub!

Saturday night into Sunday rituals were easy and relaxing tasks as the long week ended. KW flicked the feather duster over the old clock and put his ear to the workings to be sure the ticktock of the tavern clock was in good shape. "All is well in the heart of Nantucket," he said to Marshmallow.

KW climbed down the stepladder to rub Marshmallow's silky black and white fur. Marshmallow let out a loud yawn and stretched out on top of the bar, as content as could be.

"You know, Marshmallow, Richard was back in again. This time with his wife. She's tall, very attractive, and it's rumored that she comes from European royalty. We're moving up in the world, Marshmallow!" After the first time Richard had come in on that stormy night, the very next morning six large red wine glasses, all wrapped in protective wrap in a nice bag from Tonkins Housewares, were sitting at the back door. Then around noon a box of assorted red French wine was delivered with a note taped to it.

KW,
Keep these in your cellar for me for when I come in for dinner, and charge me plenty for each bottle. If your friend Neil comes in, tell him I would like to meet him. Pick a nice bottle from my case, and serve it to him and charge it to me. Just drop the bill off in my mailbox.
Thanks,
Richard

Who is this guy Richard? he wondered. When Dolly and Nobby, Richard's neighbors, came in for lunch a week later, KW sat down with them for a few moments and inquired about the man.

"Well," Dolly replied, "he's a very influential banking investor from Chicago and is reported to have a vast estate in Chicago and a private museum, as well, in Lake Geneva, Wisconsin. People remark that it's the largest personal home in the state. He also owns another property with a home in the Caribbean, which is rumored to be a whole mountain. His wife, breathtakingly beautiful, is actually part of the Latvian royal family and is as sweet as apple pie!"

KW set his thoughts about Richard aside. He tried to take at least every other Sunday off. Sometimes it worked; other times he worked several Sundays in a row. *Ah, life in the restaurant business,* he always thought to himself.

After all his closing chores were finished on this Saturday evening, he headed into the kitchen to pour a small saucer of milk for Marshmallow, who was following close behind, knowing there was a treat in store for her. After placing the dish on the floor for Marshmallow, KW said to himself, "Oh, Sylvia's blueberry pie."

Sylvia was the daytime kitchen cook and had worked at Cy's for as long as anyone could remember. Her blueberry pie was known all over the island as the best in town. People would go out of their way to get a slice or a whole pie to take home.

KW cut himself a generous slice of pie and added a scoop of her hand-churned vanilla ice cream. He had already poured water into the aluminum drip percolator, just enough for two cups, and waited patiently for it to finish brewing. He was enjoying his aromatic coffee and pie as he glanced through the latest edition of the *Cape Cod Crier*.

"Not much news to report, Marshmallow. Looks like last week's storm did some damage to the back road down to the ferry. There is a big church social coming up in Hyannis, and no one we know seems to have passed away. Some senator is making a speech on Wednesday at the Bandstand on the Green in Boston. How he's going to lower the taxes is the subject."

He then picked up the *Inquirer and Mirror* that had come out on Thursday. It was laying in the corner of the bar. "Well, Marshmallow, it was—and I quote—'another delightful season at Tuckernuck. It was brought to a formal close with the holding of the annual Tuckernuck Olympics at the North Head Beach a few weeks ago. Conditions were ideal for this high point of the Tuckernuck summer, with spectators and participants lending vociferous enthusiasm to each event and particularly to the climactic presentation of the Joseph Qarren Phinney Memorial Cup.' I kid you not, Marshmallow." Marshmallow just looked up at KW while rolling around on the bar countertop and let out a meow.

"Not only that, Marshmallow, an advertisement here states the coal barge *Commodore* is now unloading at Old South Wharf. 'Order your winter supply from this fresh cargo of famous Reading Anthracite. All sizes clean, well graded, direct from the mines. Deliveries promptly made. Phone Island Service Co.' Well, Marsh, we are all set. Robbie Egan loaded us up last week. We should be good to go for the whole winter!"

After he finished his late-night snack, he brought his dishes into the kitchen, snatched one of Sylvia's lemon snap cookies out of the jar, and returned to the bar for a nightcap. KW enjoyed his usual favorite, a nice Fonseca tawny port to end the night. As he put down the paper, Marshmallow curled up in the corner booth, and he spoke to her softly. "It sure feels good to sit." As KW finished his port, he continued to talk to the cat. "Did you catch any mice today, Marsh?" She did not look up or open her eyes, but he knew she was listening, as her ears perked up at the mention of her name.

One more item that KW did on Saturday evenings before he departed was a quick inventory of the liquor room. He also found an advertisement in a magazine for whiskey, and he chuckled to himself as he read it: "Whenever Kentucky hosts, serve never the most, but always the best one bottled in bond is most often the bottle in hand … In bourbon's home state, its OLD FITZGERALD: naturally distilled and aged our own one genuine sour mash formula since 1870."

"'Old Fitzgerald.' How do you think they came up with that name, Marshmallow?"

He walked over to the wall and said, "How about old KW … a fine old bottle served seasoned and creaky with age!"

KW smoothed the ad onto the wall in the liquor room and taped it up. It pictured a graceful southern mansion covered in ivy. A gilt key floated above the text. It was a tasteful ad, not like some of the garish ones he had seen in the past in the windows of liquor stores in the big cities.

Nantucket folk were not the type to buy gaudy things they saw in a storefront window. No, they wanted simplicity and enjoyable things in their lives to balance the enjoyable summers and the harsh winter weather.

"Maybe we'll get some fancy tourists who will partake in expensive bourbon," he said to Marshmallow. The cat just looked up from the booth and gave out a meow. "You know, Marsh, some people will believe anything they read and buy anything at times."

KW unlocked the front door, and Marshmallow gave a sniff of the air. She trotted out into the darkness for her nightly wanderings with her tail straight up in the air. KW said to himself, "She's the best mouser in town." He knew that before the night ended, she would find her way back into the restaurant via her own cat door that KW had installed in one of the back windows of the bar. She would curl up in a corner booth for a long sleep. With that thought, he turned off all the lights and headed out to his apartment.

The fog had started to roll in earlier and had become quite thick. The temperature was dropping. It looked like Sunday was going to be a crisp and bitter one. A northeast wind had been blowing all day and there was not much sun poking through the clouds.

Even with Sunday being his only day off, there were two things that made him stop by the restaurant. One of them was Sylvia's freshly made sugar doughnuts that she offered only on Sunday mornings, and they sold out quickly. She would make 140 for restaurant patrons and 60 for takeaway with a limit of 6 per request. She often thought about hiring a helper on Sundays to increase the number of doughnuts for takeaway, but it never seemed to transpire.

The restaurant opened up at 10:00 a.m., and almost every Sunday there was a line for the takeaway of the doughnuts.

KW would head down to Cy's for a quick doughnut and a cup of coffee, never sitting at the bar but standing in the kitchen with Sylvia. She truly enjoyed their conversations. They would discuss new menu ideas and any special requests for the weekly kitchen inventory.

Later on in the afternoon he would head back to Cy's for the Sunday blue plate special. Today's offering was a generous slice of Sylvia's five-spiced slow-roasted pot roast, which she would always prepare one day prior, as the true flavor came forth after a day of sitting in the natural juices, and then she would add the final touches to make the delicious gravy. It was served with buttermilk mashed potatoes and warm, flaky rolls. This was a standard Sunday special that ran from 11:00 a.m. until the kitchen closed or when they sold out. KW would enjoy it while sitting at the horseshoe bar, always engaging in conversation with others that he knew so well or perhaps a new customer just out on a day trip or a few days' visit.

This week he also had to get together with Hoody and Donna, two of his bartenders. They were going to be taking care of the Tom Nevers Fishing Club on Monday. Neil Krauter was hosting the event. Krebs, who was in charge of the menu ideas, told KW and Sylvia Neil would bring in some freshly caught bass for the main dish. There would be about twenty to twenty-four persons in total. He asked

Sylvia if they could set up a large iced container and stock it with Budweiser, Pabst Blue Ribbon, and Ballantine beers. Neil had told KW, "Make sure you have a couple bottles of good red wine available, and just house charge the whole evening to me. Add a nice tip. Put it on my house charge. This one doesn't go on my barter system. I will bring an envelope of cash to you the next day." They also needed to have some regular house wines available. In addition, Neil requested a couple platters of sliced meats and cheeses. With large self-serve bowls of salad and vegetables they were good to go. They will serve everything family style.

Krebs had a glass of red wine in his hand the whole time. Everyone at the restaurant seemed to know him— customers and employees alike. KW could not remember the last time Krebs ever had to pay for a drink. Before he departed he went into the kitchen, gave Sylvia a hug, had a wee dram of blackberry brandy, and headed out.

KW would make it a short visit today. A glass of the house red wine to enjoy with dinner, and then he was out the door. He worked so many hours there. It was good to be away. *But how can you pass up Sylvia's food? Almost impossible!* he thought.

KW enjoyed reading and looked forward to his Sundays of peace and tranquility on his comfortable couch in his second-story apartment with a great view of the harbor. Business had been so brisk. After only six months of ownership, his revenue was up an easy 40 percent over the sales of the past owners.

The Slimmons had left him a ledger that they kept with their sales and notes on the weather and the number of lunches, which stopped at 3:00 p.m. Dinner count started after that. They left it for him to do comparisons.

KW had little time to settle down and catch up on the latest news or the island gossip, except for what he heard round the bar or from the waitresses who worked at the tavern.

Neil loved to hang around with Krebs. One day they were taking a long afternoon in a back booth. Neil was trying to get the damp cold off his bones, as he had been out fishing with Bubba on the beach on Eel Point since mid morning. Krebs said while enjoying a very good glass of wine, "Every time I see you headed somewhere I swear you're with a different woman. I hear the guys joking around, calling you Romeo!"

"It's the life one has to lead, Krebs old boy!"

"So how did you get such wealth? Was it family inheritance?"

"No," Neil replied, "I had a good childhood, great family. My family has been in the insurance business since the 1890s, so I started working it when I was sixteen. Then I had visions. My uncles, father, brothers, everyone thought I was delusional, but I had my secretary help me start following my dream. It wasn't easy, as she was tied to my father for weekly reports on my personal dealings with clients.

"So what was your dream?" Asked Krebs.

"Well, I drafted a letter, redrafted, worked it over and over. I bet I redid it forty times until I thought it was perfect. And at the same time I placed a similar advertisement in Chicago; New York; Boston; Dallas; Houston; Miami; Washington, DC; New Orleans; San Francisco; Seattle; Vancouver; Toronto; Minneapolis; and several other cities that repeated every fourteen days on Sunday and ran for three months straight. I sent out the letters once a week. I typed them on our new stationery I designed just for this venture, a serious bold, gold letterhead I had made at the printers. The top center read 'Krauter Investments and Insurance,' with all the Krauter names underneath in black—six on one side, six on the other side at the top of the page." "So what happened?" Krebs asked, pouring another glass of red wine.

"Well, the first letter I sent out was to the actor James Stewart, next one to Gary Cooper, followed by Cary Grant, Humphrey Bogart, Henry Fonda, Orson Welles, Gregory Peck, Bing Crosby, Alec Guinness, James Cagney, Fred Astaire. I also sent one to Governor Poletti from New York, Governor Saltonstall from Massachusetts, our president of the United States hopeful Franklin D. Roosevelt. I included several museums, like the Guggenheim. Then I reached out to Henry Ford, the Vanderbilts, Carnegie Mellon, the Rockefeller family. I also contacted the railroad unions, the US Department of Agriculture, and the US Defense Department.

Over 80 percent of them finally came our way, investing in our ideas, insuring their properties and their personal investments. Word spread like wildfire throughout the Cinema Guild Unions that we were the solid investment in troubled times. And the rest is history! My father and relatives were astounded when the first response came in from James Stewart, and the letter was addressed to me. Then almost like clockwork, every ten to twenty days another reply would arrive addressed to me. I arranged all the meetings, always traveling to them unless they were in New York, and coming back with a huge investment and a 'Broker of Record' transfer. I took our company up well over a hundredfold in about two years, and that was just the tip of the iceberg!"

"Wow, that's really amazing." Krebs replied.

Herman Melville commented on Nantucket's whaling dominance in his novel Moby-Dick.

CHAPTER THREE

Saturday was KW's longest shift at Cy's. His day began at 9:00 a.m. to prepare for the ten o'clock breakfast crowd. Sylvia was always there long before KW arrived. She would insist that KW have a proper breakfast before he started his day. She loved to cook for him—eggs, Irish bangers, honey maple bacon, and thick-cut toast with a piping hot cup of coffee. She knew once the doors were unlocked and they opened for business, his next break would not be until late afternoon or early evening. Nantucket became KW's full-time home, and he truly loved it, but it was not an easy place to run a pub. By the time breakfast was cleaned up, the lunch crowd would start to trickle in. There was a small, quiet break between lunch and the late-afternoon bar patrons, which would flow straight into dinner. Then the fishermen would arrive off the water, and the night would continue until the late evening hours.

KW felt as though at times he lived at the tavern. That's why he never moved into the three-room lodging above the restaurant. He needed to step away. It was a short stroll home to his rented apartment on Fair Street. He was far enough away but easily accessible to the restaurant.

As Monday rolled around, KW felt refreshed after a nice day off. He could make any work schedule he wanted. He enjoyed his job, so he chose to work a six-day week most often from late June through mid-September. It was a seasonal island, and it slowed down quite a bit in wintertime, and so did the work hours.

On Mondays, KW's shift began at 3:00 p.m. Often showing up earlier, he chatted with Sylvia about the breakfast and lunch business. She said things were quiet because of the rain. But as soon as he put on his apron, the door just seemed to keep opening by the guests walking in.

The bar started to fill up rapidly with big burly men wearing worn peacoats and wool sweaters. They anchored up to the bar to warm and thaw their bones from being out on the open sea.

The tavern soon smelled of heavy denim pants turning damp and steamy in the heat of the room. There was a sizzle and crack from the wood in the potbellied stove as the fire warmed the air and turned the men from frozen and weather-beaten grizzly forms to warm and moving humans again.

KW often thought these fishermen were mythical. In the first early days when he acquired the tavern, he started to study them mentally. He knew they were the bread and butter of the bar. After every great catch they were flush with cash and they spent it like the old saying goes, "like a drunken sailor."

KW was grateful for their business and treated them all fairly and honestly. As the bar started to fill, there was a soft kind of silent peace, while the whiskey was poured and the coffee was replenished. Mugs and spoons clanked softly. Hats came off. Hair spiked up and out. They were like sea Gods settling down on land for the evening with their mortal families.

The wives, mothers, sons, and daughters were damn lucky to have them back on dry land and back amongst the living. These men were isolated when they were out on the great deep waters of Nantucket Sound. Living on such a tiny island away from the normal comings and goings of everyday life and the hustle and bustle of the real world wasn't the average. Many of them had families on the island, on Cape Cod, or in New Bedford. They sailed and searched for the fish, scallops, and clams; captured them; and worshipped them to a degree—the way a man respects a thing that might take his life, pulling him down into the inky depths of the sea in a minute.

KW thought of the history book he had read and how that had an influence on his life. It was a history book from 1835 by one Obed Macy called *The History of Nantucket* (first edition) that had actually drawn him to Nantucket.

Christopher Hussey killed the first spermaceti whale taken by the Nantucket Whaler. He was cruising near the shore for right whales and was blown off course some distance from the land by a strong northerly wind. When he fell into a pod of that species of whales, he killed one and brought it ashore. At what date this adventure took place is not fully ascertained, but people believe it was around 1712.

KW read that piece and fell in love with the idea of a man blown off course and sailing into a pod of whales. As a child, he had loved the story of Jonah and the whale—more so, of course, Pinocchio. Somehow just the thought of an animal big enough to engulf a whole man alive in its belly seemed so real to KW, even though he knew it wasn't possible. Or was it?

As he became older, KW thought of going out to sea to capture one of these giants and hauling it back to land. Well, it would never happen. It was the stuff from which legends and stories of the Gods were derived, about which novels and myths were written—the men and the isolated island of Nantucket.

As KW tended to the men at the bar, he studied them, looking at their windburned faces and callous hands that seemed to glow and speak of their rough lives out on the open seas. He got to know more personal information about everyone new who ventured into the bar—where they lived, some things about their family, who taught them about the fisherman's trade, and the forefathers who all worked hard.

For an outsider looking into the restaurant through the burnished glass windows, these rough-looking men looked tired and miserable. Their backs were bent with exhaustion. Their hands were knotted from years of tossing nets and winding winches. Their legs, if they could be seen, would show them to be crooked and bowed from the dip and bend of the sea, from working the fishing trawlers. But if you asked any of them why they did not do a different type of less stressful work, they would tell you, "Once the sea is in your veins it never escapes you. It's all we have ever known or worked."

Walking around the horseshoe bar, swiping his rag over the counter, pouring fresh beers and mugs of hot refreshing coffee and spikes of Jameson, KW would hear bits and pieces of so many conversations. He sometimes felt as if he was stitching together the patchwork of their existence. Sometimes it would all come together in his mind, and other times it wouldn't.

"Two-thirds of the cantankerous globe is the Nantucketers. For the sea is his, he owns it, as emperors own empires."

"She had her all hushed up there in the corner."

"Two knots."

"Sally and John ... two bits and four ..."

"Came in before the nor'easter. Did you, John?"

"We didn't get much of a catch yesterday ..."

"I heard old Trevor Smith's boys had a good run of cod late afternoon off the coast of Tuckernuck, and they are hauling their lobster traps in really early tomorrow morning. Heard him say they were headed out at 4:00 a.m. if seas calm down a bit."

"Trevor and his crew feel right at home here on the rock. They mentioned that it feels like they're back home off the coast of Devon, England. Plymouth, I believe, or Dartmouth is where their family hails from. All lay directly on the North Sea, if I remember correctly."

Man-gods eating and back with the living. Bent, kinked, and thawing out. Ancient and old before their years.

The men had been trawling and fishing and living on the seas, as some men were meant to live—away from their women and children for days on end, some truly missing the warm comfort of their homes. Whether it was on the Cape or on Nantucket, the ones who lived off island were invited many times to stay with their fellow mates in their homes. Others admitted only to themselves that they did not know any life other than out at sea. The solitude of the boat was what a true Nantucket fisherman's soul needed.

KW knew why many men chose to fish and live on the island instead of the more genteel Cape Cod: solitude and moments of sanity. Sometimes a man just needed to fade away. He needed to leave the past and history on the mainland. Sometimes a man's loss was so deep and so great that nothing and no one but the vast open sea could keep him sane.

KW stayed on Nantucket for that very reason. He did not like cities. He loved the sea and the quaint town of Nantucket. This was something only he knew and held in his heart. However, the sea had taken his love, so he remained on the dry land with his compatriots. He worked day and night. He felt that the owner should have a big presence in any type of business, and Cy's was one where you connected with your guests. You built relationships with friends and families, adding more each time a new customer entered.

KW had learned many stories from his customers about their new children, grandchildren, weddings, break ups, hardships, businesses, and many other dealings. He learned many stories of the sea from the fishermen who sat around the warm, cozy horseshoe bar, the very same bar he had acquired just over six months ago. He had remodeled it with the help of some handymen he knew who were more than happy to claim that they built the bar and were already claiming their respected seats on opening day. They transformed it from a small straight bar counter that faced a wall of liquor bottles to a horseshoe-shaped conversation pit where everyone loved to tell stories. He listened, laughed, and commented as he served up Kentucky bourbon, Irish whiskey, schnapps, some Tia Maria, a brandy, imported rum, or a warming snifter of Grand Marnier.

The last few days had been rough on all fronts. The storm blowing down from Newfoundland brought along eight- to twelve-foot swells. It also was accompanied by a gloomy, chilly downpour that flooded the streets with huge puddles. Marshmallow had begun her usual routine.

She got up in the morning and ventured out in the nasty weather only to return a few minutes later, soaking wet and scratching at the swinging kitchen door for a saucer of milk. KW used to laugh and say, "Marshmallow, you have Sylvia wrapped around your little paw." Then Marshmallow would come out of the kitchen and sneak upstairs, where KW had placed a pillow directly in front of an old bay window overlooking Water Street. Marshmallow would curl up like she did not have a care in the world and doze off.

Even anglers of solitude and wisdom could get down in the mouth after rocking it out in the wet seas with not much of a catch to be had. Some chose to just stay tied up or moored in the harbor and wait it out, either bunking on the boat if that was possible or taking a room at Ms. Frechette's boardinghouse. She had good clean, cheap rooms on Broad Street close to the restaurants and bars.

Their clothes were damp with rain, and the thick fog did not allow much warmth for the bones of their body. Lines were hard to handle and slick with rain and oils, their soaked gloves cutting into their skin. Raw boned pain was what days like these could and did bring.

There was a trio of fishermen that had entered the bar around 4:00 p.m. It was their second time this week that they had come in shortly after lunchtime. For lunch they started with pitchers of beer and bowls of hearty, thick clam chowder and slabs of warm buttered bread. Then they all ordered the braised beef special served with hearty vegetables and a rich, thick gravy. They sat at one of the old round oak tables in the front corner by the window overlooking Water Street as the rain came down sideways and pelted on the windowpanes.

KW had never seen these men before this week, but there were times when men were out on their trawlers and felt it was easier to haul up in Nantucket Harbor than to head back to the Cape in bad weather. They peeled off their wet coats and hats and settled in. The special for lunch was Ms. Sylvia's slowly braised beef in a rich brown sauce with carrots and peas served atop thick-cut garlic bread. They jumped right on it for the second time that week.

One of the fisherman asked KW his name and then added, "Tell whoever this Ms. Sylvia is that this meal has hit the spot. This beef dish brings me back to land."

KW replied, "You have not lived until you've tried a piece of her blueberry pie."

How could they resist a slice of her supposedly famous pie? It was served warm and topped with her hand-churned vanilla ice cream. A round of coffees with Jameson added to it topped off their second visit for lunch.

"A big salute to Sylvia." They all clinked their glasses together.

KW nodded in agreement. "I couldn't do without her cooking. That's for sure. For that matter, many people on this island would not fare as well either."

As they warmed themselves, KW kept an eye on them, making sure the beer and liquor was flowing. He knew when new guests were treated well they became repeat customers time and time again. "Tried and true!"

KW figured they must have gotten a decent catch even in this cold, dreary weather or earlier in the week. There was cash and coin, and they were willing to spend it freely. That was the nature of the beast.

One of the men introduced himself as Tristram. He ordered a newfangled beer that KW was now stocking called Schlitz. KW had begun carrying it in July, because he liked the advertisement he saw one day while in Hyannis.

It seemed to go over quite well. The advertisement had showed a group of men all sitting around a campfire accompanied by three willowy women, preparing food on a large table. "A real adventure in good living. Just kiss the hops ..."

The beer went over well with mainly the offshore fishermen who stopped in. He thought maybe they had seen it in the Cape Cod bars, so he kept it available despite his penchant for Budweiser.

"KW, can you fetch me another Schlitz?"

"Whiskey will warm your belly faster," he replied. With that, he held up the Jameson bottle and wiggled it around.

"I'm thirsty, KW! That salt air's got me all parched. It's got my skin and my throat all dried up!"

"Sure thing, Tristram," replied KW as he handed a cold bottle of Schlitz over to him. *A fisherman knows what he wants, and he will have it,* thought KW.

Swordfish, cod, hake, haddock, squid, or sole on any given day—the golden weight of the catch was enough to make or break a man's back or bank. It was all in the belly of the sea. No ifs, ands, or buts; no amount of cajoling, and no prayer was going to save a man from his fate at sea. Once land bound, the men would opt to control what little they could, like food and drink—surely not the women. Still a man could try to control his fate.

KW was more than a little familiar with the ways of these men, as he had fished with his father up and down the coast from Gloucester to New Bedford. His father had been sucked into the magical tales of succulent scallops and shellfish. "There's gold in the Sound off the coast of Nantucket," he would say many times in his life. His friend reeled him to the fishing life. KW's father bought a small trawler and started exploring the deepwater canyons off the coast of the island.

His father had taken him out many times on overnight trips on the small trawler and felt after getting used to the trips out at sea, it was better to invest in a larger, more seaworthy boat and to find a crew of two more to join and fish with him.

KW loved the excitement of the trips and learned to enjoy the solitude of being out on the open sea. He always had felt so safe with his father on these trips in his battered peacoat, rain hat, and gum boots. His dad made him wear foul weather gear. He always wore a life preserver, as he had promised both his parents. His father's sense of caution was overwhelming at times. If it was looking like a storm might blow in, KW was not allowed to go. He didn't like being left behind, but deep inside he understood the reason.

His father loved the ocean, Hyannis, and Nantucket Sound but was in no way blinded by the siren's call. He knew of the stories by Melville and Hemmingway. "Old Man Sea could be heartless. He could snatch a person from a deck without a moment's notice, carry him out to sea, and pull him under to a watery tomb!"

KW thought back to a conversation when he was a child with his father after they had obtained their first trawler: "Kenny, don't ever believe you're better than the sea. It commands respect and constant thinking. Don't believe all the storytellers unless you read between the lines."

"What do you mean, Papa?" KW would ask even though he knew what he meant. He had listened to his father's familiar hodgepodge of philosophy for many of his young years. His father quoted Melville, which he loved to add to conversations.

"Nantucketers overran and conquered the water world like so many Alexanders," his father would say, "as if we could tame a thing like the sea. As if we could rope her down like a young calf. See, Kenny, those are just myths. We are not Gods. We are ants in the belly of the beast!"

KW, around twelve at the time, just nodded to his father and began thinking about what they were going to have for dinner as they headed back to shore and the warmth of the house.

Now in his real life, he would give anything to be back out on the sea in their trawler with his father. "Just one last time," he would say to himself. "One last time!"

Nantucket Clam Chowder (from an old recipe found in Cy's kitchen)
   1 large white onion
   1½ cups celery, chopped
   2 tbs butter
   1/4 cup flour
   6 cups 2% milk
   ½ cup clam juice
   3 cups fresh clams, chopped
   1 bay leaf
   1 cup potatoes, diced and cooked

Sauté onion and celery in butter until softened. Add milk and clam juice. Gradually sift in flour. Stir well to avoid clumping. Do not let it boil. Add potatoes, bay leaf, and clams. Simmer for 30–45 minutes. Serve with warm toasted bread.

Nantucket probably takes its name from Wampanoag word that translates as "Natocke."

CHAPTER FOUR

The next day KW said pretty much the same thing to Cooker about one more trip on the sea with his father. They were enjoying a nice hot roast turkey lunch with all the trimmings in the Napoleon Room at the Chanticleer Inn and Restaurant located in Sconset.

Jeffrey Cook was an up-and-coming playwright. He already had three plays on Broadway under his belt and no intention of slowing down. Cooker was born in Portsmouth, New Hampshire, but traveled down to the island with his family in the summer. They had a summer home, ironically enough, on a lane named Broadway a couple blocks from the Chanticleer Inn.

Cooker's room was above the garage. It had a large double-hung window that faced the sea. He always used to tell people who looked out of it to the ocean, "Next stop three thousand miles away: the Canary Islands." Because of the way his window was positioned, one would see the first sunlight in the United States. He would add, "That bridge next to the Sundial House is always full of people who come to Nantucket to look out at the sea for the first sunlight in America on New Year's Day! That's a fact."

All the ladies who he would bring to his humble abode would just melt away, looking at the view. He could woo them with his stories and his steel gray-blue eyes.

Cooker started out doing some summer plays on the island and soon found himself at parties and gatherings with actors, playwrights, investors, and directors. Many of them seemed very enthralled with the young man.

One such actor named John asked him if he would like to join him on a trip to New York to watch him perform in a play on Broadway. His friend John's acting and the way the crowd were hanging on his every word during the play mesmerized Cooker.

Cooker went back to New York to his friend John again one fall after spending the summer on Nantucket. Cooker asked John if he could hang out for a few weeks and finish his screenplay that he was toying around with the past few months while on the island. John set him up in his spare bedroom with a desk and typewriter and gave him the writer's lecture: "Remember—no matter what you have going on, you *must* write at least one page a day. It's the golden rule to getting your story finished. No exceptions!"

The story he laid out for John sounded oh so familiar: a small beach town with lots of skeletons in the closet. John let out a good chuckle and replied, "If Hunter were here, he would say, 'Cookie, only you could come up with that story!'"

Two years later it ran on Broadway for fourteen months. The play was underwritten by Krauter Company, and Neil Krauter managed to bring no less than ten beautiful women to enjoy the show from their private box seats.

It was simply titled *Island Gossip*, and that was his start in the playwright field.

"Remember those days when we were kids when we used to go out on the trawler with my pa?" KW pushed his fork full of turkey and stuffing around his plate, sopping up the gravy and the last of the cranberry sauce. "You should write about that sometime."

Cooker was not a man of many spoken words. He just shook his head and shrugged. "Not enough dirt. No sex. No murder. There's no mystery. No housekeepers having sex with their rich employers in the guest cottages of their mansions. No mystery to it. It's got to have some guts. No guts, no glory," he stated.

KW looked solemnly out the windows of the restaurant at the trees that were swaying back and forth. The nor'easter they had been talking about was starting to move in. It seemed like it had been forever starting to brew.

It was around two in the afternoon. The skies were getting darker and more gray with each passing minute. KW noticed that the sand on the street was blowing around, as well. He thought to himself, *Hope Marshmallow found her favorite spot, up on the second floor by the front window ledge of the restaurant, to hang out.*

"Come on, Cooker. Why don't you write something nice and decent that everyone could enjoy? As it is now, people won't even bring their kids to one of your plays."

"In New York people don't bring their kids to plays on Broadway. They only do that around the holidays when they see *Wizard of Oz* or a Christmas-style play," Cooker replied. Then out of nowhere Cooker said, "I think I have been drinking too much." And with that said, he finished off his glass of red wine with a silly smirk on his face.

"That's the first true thing you have said during this entire meal." KW laughed.

"I love coming back to the island. Long lunches with friends, a big fat nap, and a little writing. The salt air and the fall are some of my favorite things out here. The tourists are gone, and we can all spend some time hanging out. The train out to Sconset is almost empty. It's peace and solitude until mid-December, when it's time to bail back to the city." Then Cooker went into one of his daydreams. His steel-gray eyes were lost in thought, which usually lasted three or four minutes. KW just watched, as he had in the past, wondering what he was dreaming of now—a new play idea or the last roll in the hay with some tourist girl.

When Cooker finally returned from his trance, KW spoke. "It sure is, Cooker. It sure is. Things are slowing down. Even for me at the bar. I'm grateful for all the summer tourists and their business. We've managed to build quite a solid reputation this season at Cy's. It was such a great move for me to take the leap and buy the business, and now I'm working on buying the building. Like you said, the late fall is good for one's mind and soul!" KW spoke as if he was fading off into a dream himself. "Oh, I almost forgot to tell you. Rusty and I drew up the plans for your new pad above the bar. It's going to be sweet! It's being designed to be a one-bedroom, sixteen by eighteen, which is a really good size. It will have a full-sized closet with a galley-style kitchen, a full bath, and another half bath. There's also going to be another smaller room, ten by fourteen, for a den or writing space. Kinda exciting, huh? We got approved to add three sets of double-paned windows for more light. I know how depressed you get in the dark," joked KW.

Cooker just grinned and rolled his eyes. "We're also gonna redo the stairwell going up from the back of the restaurant with a much nicer, more secure winter door to the outside. The window that's in the hall—you know where Marshmallow likes to laze around—is gonna stay the same."

"God forbid we renovated Marshmallow's window," Cooker said with a throaty laugh.

"She would have a fit!" KW added, enjoying a good laugh, as well.

"You mean to tell me that old Riddleburger is back? I thought he headed down to Florida. The last time I was here he was doing a huge renovation job in Quidnet for Geno, and then he said he was going to try the Florida life for a while. Don't his parents have a place on the ocean near Jacksonville? You remember he was always trying to get us to go down there when Nantucket was like a frozen tundra in January?" Cooker asked.

"Yup, he's back. Came up in August. Said Florida was like an oven so he's going to try to do a split season, here and Florida. His parents are thrilled to have a bit of peace and quiet, and we're all glad to have him back. That man can fix anything! Give him a screwdriver, hammer, and saw, and he can build a palace! You're going to love the apartment when it's done. That way when you want to come up to the island for a long weekend you won't have to take that cold train ride out to Sconset. The bad part is I think Marshal is really going to miss you. The train is so empty for most of the winter rides. For him, I think he gets lonely. He loves to talk with anyone who's on the train before they depart and after they arrive to their stop. The man is an encyclopedia of island history. You know he's been the conductor on that train for as long as I can remember ..." KW trailed off.

"I can't wait to see the drawings for the new apartment. It's still, like you said, a long slow train ride out to Sconset. And after mid-October the wind will just whip off the coast right through my garage apartment. Some mornings the heat just can't keep up above the garage, so I have to move back into the main house. My father is always saying they needed to drain the pipes by December 1. I make them keep the heat on until mid-January. My old man still bitches about it, but I explained to him that it's when my best writing creativity happens. You know him—he loves to be front row for my plays. For that matter"—Cooker chuckled—"he likes to be in the front row of any plays I can get him tickets for. God, he loves hobnobbing with all the actors that are around. So he bends pretty easily. And he loves John Shea, as a person, director, and an actor, so when I remind him about all the plays, the trips to New York, and the famous playwrights and actors I can get him introduced to, he gives in and keeps the heat on.

"Plus, I always arrange front-row seats for my plays and John's shows, as well, and backstage champagne toasts. He just loves it, I tell ya. Loves it! My father is always chumming up to Neil when he sees him here and in Nantucket. You know money sure does some funny things to people, not excluding my father!"

"You know, Cooker, you never really can leave this island. It's magical. There is no other place like Nantucket. It can chew you up and spit you out, or you can mesh and blend in with the island folks! It's all about the fish, dressing nice on Sundays, which you seem to forget about, and now and then taking a dip off the beach in the water, if it ever gets warm enough!"

"Ain't that the truth! Sometimes we just take things for granted. I find myself in New York, daydreaming about Sconset. I get what your friend Jed, the winemaker, always calls it—writer's block—when I'm in the city. Not like here on the island. All it takes is a nice glass of his red wine to make me dream away and lose my train of thought."

"Oh yeah, now I remember. You did write about several of our island characters in that play *Island Gossip.* Everyone was taking the train to New York to see that play. I think they all went just to find out if they were a character in it. You know one of the more interesting characters in that play was Hunter Laroche. Everyone wants to know who that guy was."

"Yeah, I made him out to be the international man of mystery. Well, that's not far from the truth, KW. Laroche is a mystery. I met him years ago. I had spotted him in the Tap Room. He was off to the side at one of the tables with Krebs and Torpe, enjoying a bottle of wine and some cheese and meats. I wondered who he was. Then a short time after I see he's hanging around with Bradshaw. Another time he's with Gene Mahon, then with Geno and Riendel, so I ask Gene one day about him. Gene tells me he's a wild one. You never know where you're gonna spot him. Torpe saw him on a yacht in St. Barts. Geno ran into him at a party in Monaco in the south of France. He was staying at some duke's private residence there. Pirate Pete said, out of the blue, that he saw him on some large yacht, pulling into Little Harbor in the Abacos, and Rinedel tells me he stays in Sconset on the bluff in some mansion. I've heard Hunter and this guy Bubba, Joe's friend with that biplane, had some dealings in the Caribbean, as well. And the dealings are not for public information. Someone else told me they ran into him at Tres Hermonos Bar in Havana."

KW started to laugh. "This is a funny little island full of funny little people, and quite interesting to say the least. It was a hoot when everyone came back from the play and started more gossip. They kept saying, 'This part was about him, that part was about her.' They all just started looking at each other, as if they knew all of their dirty little secrets. It was the talk of the island. Man, Shea was so good at promoting you. It's nice to have close friends like that. It must have really helped you out in the ratings department, huh?"

"Yeah, that old Mr. Shea is a great guy. I'm lucky to have such a good friend. Everyone needs friends like that in the big city. It can get pretty rough. Neil Krauter has also become a fan and an investor, partly by yours and John's nudging! You know, good girls in pearls, bad boys in cars. Daddy's rich money! They like Duke Ellington and the gin joints. They don't want to hear about some island kid trawling for fish while his dad quotes Melville."

Cooker started humming and singing: "Have a drink on me/Whiskey, gin and brandy/With a glass I'm pretty handy/I'm trying to walk a straight line/On sour mash and cheap wine/So join me for a drink boys/We're gonna make a big noise."

KW started snapping his fingers, softly laughing. He leaned in with his glass of ginger ale and started singing along: "So don't worry about tomorrow/Take it today/Forget about the check/We'll get hell to pay/Have a drink on me/Have a drink on me/Yeah, have a drink on me/Have a drink on me!"

They started to roll with laughter. All the people had already cleared out, and they were the only two left in the Napoleon room, when in walked Hunter Laroche and Neil Krauter. "Holy shit!" Cooker started laughing. "What the hell are you doing on the island this time of year, Hunter?"

Hunter walked over to the table and pulled up a couple chairs. "Just in town for a quick visit."

"Hey, Tracy, can we get a good bottle of red wine over here?"

"Sure," Tracy replied. "How good?"

"Really good," Hunter said.

"Really, really good," Neil added.

KW looked at his watch. "Well, it's 3:00 p.m., perfect time for a glass of wine." They all started rolling with laughter.

After two bottles of Chateau Petrus, Hunter paid cash for the whole tab—their lunch, the wine, and the platter of imported cheeses.

They all walked at a brisk pace with their collars pulled up around their necks as the wind was giving a pretty good blow to the train depot—if you could call a little wood-covered shed that had two benches under a pitched roof a depot.

Marshal was just shutting the doors on the two-car train as they walked up. He said, "You guys just made it."

There were only a few other people in the front car. They had the second car all to themselves, laughing away as the train pulled out.

Marshal talked to them for a moment, stating that today was the last day for the current schedule. The train would now enter into its winter schedule. Round-trips from town would now be at 7:00 a.m., 10:00 a.m., 1:00 p.m., 4:00 p.m., 7:00 p.m., and 9:00 p.m., departing from town on those hours and returning on the following hour from Sconset.

The Nantucket Lightship was one of twelve vessels that guided ships with its beams of light through the Nantucket Shoals from 1935 to 1942.

CHAPTER FIVE

By the time they arrived at Cy's, the bar was already crowded with early diners and patrons, with a spatter of fishermen ready to spend their cash.

Cooker looked over to KW as they entered and said, "Here comes the witching hour!" He found a stool at the end of the bar near the kitchen entrance.

"What's Toner doing over there in the end seat? Looks like he's busy at work."

"Don't know."

KW replied, "Donna says he asked for a pen. He told her it was some application to Nantucket bank he had to fill out. She says he's been at it for almost an hour. All sorts of pieces of paper. He keeps looking at them and writes something on the form. Who knows? If he has one more glass of red wine, he might spill it all over the paperwork."

Cooker just started laughing. "Can you see him handing it to the clerk at the bank, all stained and smelling of red wine? What a hoot that would be. Yes, I filled this out at a bar over a plate of meatloaf and a few glasses of wine!"

"You bet," replied KW. "Story time is coming—the biggest fish, prettiest woman, highest wave." KW hung his jacket on the coat rungs next to the bar. He thought he would spend a few minutes with the patrons.

"My bourbon shipment did not arrive this week. I hope I make it until Monday afternoon. Next thing I am going to order more of is cognac. Neil is starting to order the good stuff. Otherwise I don't sell much. Last week Neil, Duff, and Wes Morris came in and downed my Grand Marnier and Hennessy cognac. Neil requested that I get some high-end cognac called Delamain. I am trying to locate it for him."

"Now that would be a story: Cy's runs out of Bourbon— they would bail out of here and head over to Mahon's joint in a second or the Skipper. There's not much loyalty when you're out of their favorite elixir," Cooker replied as he leaned back on his bar stool.

KW jabbed his thumb toward a booth past the bar where Pirate Pete was huddled up with what looked like a week's worth of newspapers and a bottle of red wine.

"Now there's a story for you, Cooker. About Pete and his family. They're like Robinson Crusoe."

At that point, Pirate Pete looked up and gave KW a nod, as if saying hi. He was wearing a thick wool button-up sweater, unshaven and with worn scuffed boots. KW knew he was drinking a great bottle of Bordeaux that he kept in stock for him.

"I have never met that guy Pete. I've heard a few things about him but don't know him personally," Cooker said as he glanced in Pete's direction.

"Well, I'll introduce you two sometime. He likes to come in to chat with Sylvia about something to nibble on. He walks right into the kitchen, and he and Sylvia have a good laugh. Sylvia always puts together a nice platter of meats and cheeses for him. He just sits in the booth and reads either the newspapers or a book. He sometimes stays for the whole afternoon or into the evening. Just like that guy Richard from Chicago."

With that, Donna, the bartender, came over to Cooker and asked, "What can I get you?"

Cooker thought for a moment and replied, "Just a glass of red wine. What's the price of that wine he is drinking?" KW giggled as he whispered the price to him. Cooker choked, "Too rich for my blood. I'll stick with the house rotgut!"

"Pete has always marched to his own drum. Doesn't bother anyone and spends good money. He gets along well with a lot of the customers here. He chats with them for a while, then heads to a booth," KW said as he looked at Pete admiringly.

Cooker took out a stub pencil from his coat pocket and a small dog-eared notebook and asked, "What's the story about him?"

He drew a whale on the beach. Then he sketched Pirate Pete just as he was in the booth with the bottle of wine on the table.

KW started to tell Cooker what he knew. "Well, Pete loves the sea. He wasn't born into it. His daddy dragged him out sailing when he was younger, off the coast of New Jersey, and he just grew accustomed to it and never looked back. There is a true story about his dad packing up the family and sailing down to the Abaco Islands in the Bahamas. I guess they squatted on some land and acquired it!"

"Never heard of those islands," replied Cooker.

"I think they are in the northern Bahamas. I remember Pete telling me a ways back. The story he told me is wild, but Hunter told me it's all true. He's known Pete for many years and has been to Little Harbor, where he lives."

"So what's he doing up here? Ain't this where all the sea nuts come and those of us who befriend them?"

"Sure is, brother, sure is. You never saw the article in the *New York Times* about Pete's dad, have you? Hunter has a copy of it, but he never gave it to me. I bet it's interesting, to say the least!" KW walked away for a minute, only to return with a bowl of peanuts in their shells and two short glasses. "Hey, Donna, grab the bottle of schnapps out of the icebox and pour Cooker and me a quick two fingers full, please."

"On the way," she said. Donna grabbed the peppermint schnapps, brought it over, and poured two nice-sized shots for them both.

"The way Hunter told me the story goes something like this …" KW chatted for a long time, telling Cooker all the details he could remember. Cooker took notes, and when he got home hours later, he wrote the story in his own words.

The True Early Days of a Pirate in the Making

They say that Pete Johnston's dad carried a crazy gene, if you know what I mean. His daddy was a professor at Princeton University for quite a good many years. He had a lovely wife, a great job, and wonderful children. He was surrounded by family and books.

Well, he got this crazy notion early one summer. He packed up some boxes and supplies, dried venison, canned goods, books, some art supplies, gallons of fresh water, sardines, crackers, salted pork—well, you get the drift.

He put everyone on his sixty-five–foot sailboat and headed down the coast toward the Caribbean. They ducked in and out of places, going down the Intracoastal Waterway.

When they got off the coast of Georgia, he unrolled a nautical map and showed his wife and kids where they were heading: the Abaco Islands off the coast of northern Florida. The kids; Pete and his two older brothers just looked with wide eyes and thought they were going on a treasure hunt. His wife had no idea what to think but loved her husband and knew he was a man with vast knowledge of the seas and many aspects of life.

After a little over three weeks, they landed in Nassau town. They spent a few days combing the beaches and strolling through the markets while Mr. Johnston went to the government offices to inquire about the islands like Hope Town, Eleuthera Island, and Marsh Harbor.

They put their sights on Marsh Harbor, which was more or less the starting ground for any sailors planning to travel around the islands. They sailed over on the third day. A good steady wind carried them smoothly without any upsets on the open ocean.

They arrived and docked in the very friendly small port of Marsh Harbor. The kids were free to roam the beaches, paths, and small streets. There wasn't really a whole lot for them to do.

Mr. Johnston chatted with a few of the boat captains who were also moored to the main dock, and after a full day he set his sights on an area about twenty miles south of Marsh Harbor called Little Harbor.

They regrouped and restocked their supplies. They were told it was an undeveloped area but made for good fishing and a safe harbor via a small 100-yard inlet opening. The next day they casted off, saying good-bye to the nice people they had met in Marsh Harbor.

About two hours later on that very calm day they spotted the inlet and sailed smoothly into the little beautiful crescent-shaped harbor. They moored about seventy-five feet out, and the kids just jumped in and swam to shore while Mr. Johnston and his wife took in their small dinghy.

Pete had an active imagination and wondered if there was any pirate treasure buried there. After they set up some tents in an area near the beach under some beautiful large trees, the kids went off in search of firewood and did some exploring along the harbor's rocks and hills.

Pete's brother headed to the inlet and started fishing, and within minutes he was reeling in some beautiful snappers.

Mr. Johnston and his eldest son would sail around to a few of the other islands, but they never managed to find a spot as safe from the open sea or as beautiful as Little Harbor.

One morning they took a boat ride together to Hope Town and found a quaint little village with some lovely homes and very friendly people living there. Deep in her heart Mrs. Johnston was hoping that this would be where they settled in a nice home that overlooked the harbor.

They remained in Hope Town for four beautiful days. On the last day Mr. Johnston rented a guest cottage so they could actually cook a dinner and take nice hot showers. The next day they pulled anchor and headed back to Little Harbor.

They spent long restful days in Little Harbor, both of them painting and sketching while the kids fished and explored the area. They would take some overnights up to the much more active port of Marsh Harbor, where there was always some sort of activity going on.

Mr. Johnston would talk to almost anyone who would lend him an ear. He wanted to gather as much information about the people and culture of the surrounding islands as possible. He was happy tinkering around on the boat, and he loved getting insights from other sailors in the marina.

He wrote long letters to other faculty members back in New Jersey, describing the island life. He was told it could take up to two months for them to reach the recipient. Other times he was happy to join his wife under the shade of a nice palm tree and read one of the numerous books they had brought with them.

They sailed to Elbow Cay a few times for lobster lunches on the beach where they snorkeled around, looking at a few old wrecks. Sometimes they spent the evening sitting around a bonfire. Other times Pete's dad would sail out by himself and just anchor off the beach, open a bottle of wine, and write in his journal. He would just sit for hours, gazing out at the sea and watching beautiful sunsets. He could also see the distant beam of the lighthouse on a clear evening.

He felt Little Harbor was where he could start the new life. He planned to make a foundry and an art gallery. His wife pointed out to him that only two other boats had moored there in the weeks that they were there. *How many people are going to shop in an art gallery?* She thought he had illusions of grandeur.

He said they could take their paintings and sculptures up to Marsh Harbor and Nassau and sell them in the marketplace. The kids could make some fun things, as well.

As August rolled around, it was time to head back for the fall term. They sailed up to Marsh Harbor, picked up some needed supplies, and retraced their southern route back up the coast to New Jersey.

The kids were excited to head back but also sad at the same time. They loved their days of fishing, exploring, catching lobsters, making nightly bonfires, and meeting new friends. They also enjoyed the adventure of sailing to other deserted islands.

When they finally were back home in New Jersey, Pete's dad called the family together and told them of his plans. He was going to give up his teaching job in the spring. He wanted to sell the house, pack up, and sail back to Little Harbor to claim the land as theirs.

The kids let out a big hurray. Mrs. Johnston just looked at her husband with her jaw dropped open.

So as the story goes, Pete's dad drafted a letter to the dean of the college with his springtime resignation. Many faculty members were quite aghast when they learned of his plans, and several came to the house and tried to get him to change his mind and persuade him to keep his family in the safe environment of Princeton.

Mr. Johnston would not budge. He told them that the world was going to hell in a handbag and that the islands were the ideal place to live. "Listen, old man, give it a couple more years up here" (this from a visiting Edinburgh colleague).

He drafted a letter to the school's student body, one to his parents, and one to their cousins and family members. He wrote letters to the town fathers and other pillars of the Princeton community, as well as the pastor of their church. They all tried to persuade him, but it fell on deaf ears. His wife's friends also tried stating what was best for her and the children but again to no avail.

Tears ensued, quiet approached, and then acceptance settled in.

As spring approached, Mr. Johnston was making lists of what to take, what to store, and what to ship to Marsh Harbor. He had a running list of inspections for the boat, supplies, and stops along the way. He wanted to be under way by June 1. The weather should be agreeable around that time of year.

He then said good-bye to his doctoral students. He purchased a nice box of Godiva chocolates for his secretary, Ms. Collins. They were her favorites. He also got her a pair of slippers to go along with them. Ms. Collins had already been tearful for the last two weeks, and this just made her cry even more. He said, "Now, Macy, it's not all that sad. Think of it as an adventure in life, and when we get settled you can come and enjoy some of the warmth and sunshine." Again tears fell from her eyes.

He spent quite a few evenings in Mendham with his mother and father and some alone time with the wife and kids, trying to explain the unexplainable. "Sometimes a man has to do what a man has to do."

Mrs. Johnston thought the idea was "preposterous" (as she said over tea at the club), but she vowed to follow her husband's dream.

When sailing day had arrived, they packed up and cast off to a group of around thirty people. After giving hugs and waving good-bye, they set sail at 7:00 a.m.

They followed the same route as the past spring, and no major events postponed their trip. When they arrived back in Marsh Harbor, Mrs. Johnston had already compiled a list, added to it, and then added more. It seemed that every time she thought she had all the items that they needed for the upcoming month, she remembered something else. Of course when she asked the boys if they wanted anything special, they all started. Daniel was first. "Root beer barrels!"

"Me too!" Jason chimed in.

"On my list, I have already added some Coca-Cola and gum for all of you." She giggled, as she knew that would make them pay attention. "And you know, Peter, your birthday is coming up. I'm not sure I can bake you a cake on the beach." Pete fussed around on his mother's lap.

Upon arrival the kids hopped off the boat and started scurrying around the docks and the beach paths, as if they had lived there for years. They chose to overnight for three days and, with their lists, began shopping for supplies. They needed far more than they had planned on.

Mrs. Johnston planned to visit Ms. Regan, who preferred to be called Jen, at the small supply store the next day. Ms. Regan remembered her and was so excited to see her that the shopping would have to wait. She invited her to what she called "a sit-down."

Jen was married to a man who repaired boat motors and was a great carpenter. He had built several homes in Nassau before they moved to the quieter life on Marsh Harbor. They were both born and raised in Nassau town.

They had opened the shop six years prior, and it became an instant hit among the people of the island.

She told Priscilla, "Listen, deary, it is not that bad. You'll be remote. That's the hardest part, but it's only a two-hour sail in calm winds to here."

That little talk didn't do much to calm her nerves. Priscilla was worried she wouldn't be able to find a doctor if the children got sick. Jen told her they had a nice forty-year-old husband-and-wife doctor team. They had been on Marsh Harbor for ten years strong.

Priscilla loved and trusted Jen. She would send all three boys—Daniel, Jason, and Pete—to the market several times during their dockage, with a list of breads and some canned goods along with things for baking and roasting, a side of beef, yeast, sugar apples, vegetables, maple syrup, onions, leeks, pepper, herbs, and some seedlings to plant tomatoes and vegetables, for example. Priscilla would tell the boys, "Give this list to Ms. Regan, and she will get exactly what we need and the correct amounts I have requested."

With three growing boys she often ran out of provisions on the boat. She had strict rules they had to follow on what they may or may not help themselves to, and they followed their mother's direction.

"Dear, how much tobacco would you like me to get for you? Remember—it will be a couple of weeks before you get back to Marsh Harbor."

By the time Priscilla had put Pete down for his nap and fed the boys and her husband lunch on the picnic tables under the shade of a few palms near the entrance of the dock, she had an epic list with both sides filled out. She was also going through the linens, pillows, and camping gear, checking for everything possible that they might require for the beginning of their new life in Little Harbor.

After their stay in Marsh Harbor, they sailed in Little Harbor. The kids again just jumped overboard and swam to the shore, laughing and racing. Little Pete was the smallest and did not stand a chance, but he swam ashore with his life preserver on like a champion!

After they set the tents, prepared the fire pit, collected extra driftwood, and made the campsite livable, the boys were off to the rock caves. Mr. Johnston shirred up the sails and secured the boat. They made several trips ashore in the dinghy with items that would not perish or be scavenged by any animals. They were in the late-afternoon sun and the only boat in the harbor for that evening.

The next day Priscilla donned her sun hat and sandals and took to exploring the area, as she had done in the past. It was strange to be in such a quiet, remote area, but it was tranquil. She thought that it was a perfect place to set up her easel and paint in the afternoon. Still not sure how she was going to cope with this rustic island living, she kept up a positive attitude. No other humans were around, just some seagulls gliding through the air. No storefronts, not much of anything. A slightly worried look came over her, and she felt a clutch in her chest. She caught her breath and put on a brave new face. This was her life, and she could cope with it. It would take some adjusting, but she knew she could do it!

Jen told her that in about a week's time she would sail down with her children and husband for a Sunday afternoon. Oh, how Priscilla hoped she was true to her word!

Later that afternoon, a forty-two–foot sloop came sailing in and moored for the night. Priscilla was delighted to see it was a fortyish-year-old couple and was happy when they came ashore. She was dying to talk to another woman. She had Pete on her lap, reading a children's book. She put him down and greeted the new guests on the shore.

They said they were sailing down from Nassau and were going to island-hop for ten days. Priscilla said she her husband, Randolph, was out exploring the island with her two other boys.

Priscilla invited them to join her and Pete for a glass of tea. It was lukewarm, as they did not have any ice. They all sat around on the logs that Randolph and the boys had made into bench-style seats. When Randolph and the boys returned, he invited all of them to join his family for dinner on the beach. They were the last visitors Priscilla saw for another two months.

And so the days began of drawing up the plans for shelter. Randolph had the idea, the vision, and the knowledge. It was Priscilla's job to manage the provisions. It wasn't easy to make them last.

And that was more or less the way Pete grew up—on the essentials of life. fresh air, common sense, and simple food.

His father developed Little Harbor into quite the small settlement with a foundry and a small open-air bar/

restaurant called Pete's Pub. Pete had told so many stories about his childhood. He didn't remember much of the first days, trudging through the brush of parts of the island. He vaguely remembered living in the cave in the rocks during bad storms that could lash out at the island for days at a time. The cave was the only shelter before his dad and the helpers he recruited from Nassau and Marsh Harbor built their first home. They soon added a foundry building, where Mr. Johnston made metal sculptures, and things progressed into quite a decent settlement.

They now had six homes of their own. Randolph also developed eight more parcels and sold them. He also had at least ten buoys for boaters to moor off and come ashore.

His mother, Priscilla, stuck by her husband and kids through thick and thin. She schooled each child for two hours a day almost seven days a week. Time wore on, and Priscilla grew weary and exhausted from the harsh environment. At times, she didn't think she could go on. Her constitution wasn't meant for all the salt, wind, and heat. She would dream about a hot bath and the makings of a normal home life within a community.

She had the children to think about; they all seemed so happy and well adjusted. After the first home was constructed, life seemed to be on a much smoother track. It was almost like they reached the end of the high rough trip up to the top of the mountains, and now she could clearly see the valleys and streams.

Jen would come visit every few weeks, sometimes bringing her children, Linus and Nola, along for the adventure. Priscilla would go up to Marsh Harbor with the kids and her husband, always wearing her one good dress, as often as time would allow. They became quite the talk of the Bahamas as the Robinson Crusoe family from America!

Many years later when Pete was eight, his mother died. That left the professor and his three boys alone in Little Harbor.

Word of this wild professor soon spread all over the Caribbean and the Bahamas. Boaters who moored in the safety of Little Harbor were quite impressed to see the everyday goings-on with Mr. Johnston and his children. They were still schooled daily by Randolph and had set chores and duties to be performed. People were pleasantly surprised by their knowledge and polite manners.

Pete's father had always taken a strong hand toward education, and with the passing of his wife he knew he had to stay strong and maintain the high road. The thought of moving back to Princeton crossed his mind briefly but was not ever acted upon.

Every evening he would read some quotes from famous times in history while having dinner. Late afternoon he found was the best time to have them do their reading studies and mathematics that he had planned for the week. Randolph found that early mornings were much better suited for getting tasks and building projects done and then taking a break for some swimming or a rest, a nice lunch, and then completing one more hour of tasks. An afternoon snack, then hit the studies.

They became the talk of the islands. People would cruise to Little Harbor just to meet and talk with them. A reporter from the *New York Times* even came down to the harbor to interview Randolph and the boys. They considered Randolph a "mildly eccentric local celebrity." This made it to the front page on two different occasions.

It was a quiet day in Princeton, New Jersey. Priscilla's brother, John Hayes, and his wife were reading their mail. They were very excited to finally receive a letter from

Randolph. Mrs. Hayes hurriedly opened the envelope and started reading out loud to John. They hadn't heard from Randolph since Priscilla had passed away. Pete was now around ten years old. Mrs. Hayes read the following paragraph:

> Young Pete with his wild blondish curly hair and tanned body could almost be mistaken for a young wild caveman on a deserted island. Then he speaks to me in a clear voice and strong mind of quotes from Shakespeare and asks about certain periods of history. He is so curious. He is filled with questions like "How does the stock market work?" and "Can I learn to build a boat's engine from scratch?"

Mrs. Hayes stopped reading. She had tears in her eyes. "How can this former upstanding family have gone so crazy? Or have they just turned into what the island has turned them into?"

Mr. Hayes said, "That's it! We have to save those children."

When Uncle Hayes arrived unannounced with his servants, cooks, and maid, he told Randolph straight out that this was no life for the children and he was going to take them back with him to Princeton. This started a small two-day war between the groups.

The kids did not intend to leave, and Randolph had no desire to follow suit either, but they agreed that the two eldest brothers could go back to boarding school for part of the year if they wanted.

Pete, the youngest, stood his ground. Hayes had never seen such manners from a ten-year-old boy. He was pleasant, well mannered, wild-looking, but precise and educated, which baffled Uncle Hayes. It was almost useless arguing or trying to reason with Pete and his brothers. Even more stubborn was Randolph.

Pete's brothers never really got over the fact that their mother was gone. They knew it was the hardships of the island that added to her death. They did agree to accompany Uncle Hayes and his staff back to Princeton with the understanding that they could return to Little Harbor whenever they requested to do so, as long as a member of Hayes's household staff accompanied them.

Randolph succumbed to this agreement. He was a man who loved freedom of will.

Now that Pete's brothers were back in boarding school, he was more or less alone with his father. Occasionally people would moor their boats in Little Harbor, or tradesmen would come to work on different buildings that Randolph had designed. Pete continued his schooling and had a lot of free time on his hands. He used this time to roam different islands in the area, always wearing his life preserver. He had to remain close to the shoreline and never to go out past sunset.

Pete learned to handle the dinghy well and studied the sea while he was out, watching the shore, the tides, and the waves so as not to be surprised by a sudden huge wave or to be drawn out to the deeper waters.

He and his father were working on an old larger skiff that they bought from a salvage yard in Marsh Harbor and towed back to the island. Pete missed his brothers. He missed working on some projects together, studying, horseplaying in the water, exploring the different islands and deserted beaches, fishing in different coves, and exploring the caves under the cliffs.

The dinghy became his best outlet and distraction. He would head out to one of the islands and stock up on scrap wood every morning if the seas were calm. He would make it one of his chores. Sometimes he would bring as much as three loads of wood a day—nice dried driftwood that he would paint things on and sell in the foundry.

Randolph helped Pete with his art and was quite pleased with the sales of his work. Even though there was a lot of wood where they lived, Pete enjoyed the adventure of exploring the other islands. He found many shipwrecks off the rocky coast of one of the islands. He found a small safe passage to the one area of the beach. The first few attempts were tricky, but after the fourth time he mastered it— something that he was quite sure not many skilled boatmen could accomplish. Pete could slip the boat in and out when the tides were just right.

During the first year of his brothers' departure, the professor made a few trips to Nassau to request the proper paperwork for acquiring the unforgiving land from the British government. As of now, he was living freely on the land, also known as squatting, making improvements with his own blood, sweat, time, labor, and earnest money.

It was a long drawn-out process, but he did it all properly. No one in Nassau had any interest in this unknown, almost uncharted land. The government needed a description of the land and sent a commissioned surveyor. He needed a guide from Marsh Harbor to find Little Harbor. The guide was a friend of Randolph's who admired what he had accomplished in the harbor. On the trip he chatted with the surveyor, who had a few questions about the area. The guide wanted to see Randolph acquire the land. He did not let on that he even knew Randolph. His friend painted a pretty bleak picture of the area and added mosquitoes, huge spiders, snakes, and wild boar to the conversation and told the surveyor in not so many words that "the government should be glad to rid of it!"

The surveyor met with Randolph and Pete. Needless to say, he was a little jumpy after the ride and the story of the snakes and so on. He looked around for not even thirty minutes and said he was ready to depart.

In three weeks' time a letter from the British government in Nassau arrived addressed to a Mr. Randolph Johnston. The government had no such interest in the property described as "Bound on the north by the top of Crows Peak, to the east by the rock cliffs, to the south by Wretched Crag and to the west by oceans edge."

The letter stated that Mr. Johnston could acquire it for a decent size, but very reasonable amount, of gold or coin. After payment was received and Mr. Johnston appeared in the Magistrate's Office of Documented Signatures, the property would be recorded and titled "PROPERTY OF RANDOLPH JOHNSTON, LITTLE HARBOUR, RECORDED IN NASSAU BAHAMAS BY THE QUEEN OF ENGLAND, QUEEN'S SEAL DATED."

Pete and his father continued working the land and the foundry. Daniel, his eldest brother, rejoined them to live on the island. Pete took to the island more and more as he matured. He learned everything he could about navigation by compass and sextant to the stars. He could name almost every star known to man. Pete now had fully refurbished a fifty-four–foot sloop named the *Priscilla*, after his mother. He flew the flags of the Bahamas and America, as well as a pirate flag. Pete would head out on trips sometimes for almost up to a month. These adventures took him to many islands. He would comb through open-air markets, looking for books, magazines, and other things of interest. Pete would load up with history books, things he found in the marketplaces, and things he thought his father would enjoy: supplies, tools, dried prosciutto legs, newspapers, and magazines. His father really looked forward to hearing all about his pirating adventures.

They had a nice settlement built up in Little Harbor.

Pete had picked the point where the boats entered the harbor between the hard, course rocks and built a beautiful sturdy home. It had a direct view of the ocean second to none.

The year Pete turned eighteen, his father's health was failing and he remembered the words his father spoke several years before: "Treat the sea with respect, and you will gain her confidence!" He would say, "It's the elements of good hard living finally taking its toll on my body." Pete spent more time in Marsh Harbor with his father, knowing that things were not going too well for him. Now that he was considered an adult and Randolph knew that Pete's knowledge and wisdom were way advanced for anyone near his age or even many years his senior, he knew it was time to have a serious discussion with Pete. It happened a week prior to his death.

Randolph spent over a month prior contacting a barrister in Nassau to determine the fine details on how Pete and his brothers would own the properties. He also wrote letters to each of them about how he expected them to continue, what to watch for, and what to expect after his passing.

Pete made a solemn promise to his father that he would keep the foundry running and would add a mooring a month to the harbor until they reached what they thought was workable forty-five. He promised to extend the pier. Randolph explained that he would need to contact Mrs. Ethel's sons to help him complete the task. He had set envelopes of cash in their old secure one-ton safe in the foundry office. That night after Randolph felt he had gone over every detail and had everything in order, they enjoyed a bottle of wine together. Pete consumed two-thirds of it, as his father could not find the will to drink more than a small glass. Later that evening, Randolph Winship Johnston passed away in a peaceful slumber.

Pete buried him on a grassy knoll that overlooked the foundry, the harbor, and the sea right next to his mother's grave.

There was a huge turnout for Randolph's funeral. People came from all over the islands and some from the States; even the head magistrate and a group of six from Nassau were there for a celebration of his life. Uncle Hayes and a staff of six also attended his funeral.

The cobblestones that make up some of Nantucket's streets were used by empty whaling ships as ballasts from overseas trips, returning empty to the island.

CHAPTER SIX

"Good morning, Mr. Toner. My name is June Hutton, the loan adviser here at Nantucket Bank. I reviewed your application, and there seem to be a few questions that we have to clear up. First off, I see you worked for Ruby Wines in Boston for six years, and then there is a two-year absence in any work history. I also noticed that your house mortgage is through Pacific National Bank, and I'm wondering if you're seeking to relocate the mortgage to our bank. Or are you applying for a loan? You don't have much equity in your home as of now, if it's a loan you're seeking with us."

Denis looked at her and said, "Ms. Hutton—"

"Please call me June," she replied.

"I am seeking a loan of $3,500. Things have been slow for my work at the Ocean House. I've been the manager for the dining room for over a year now. It was a quiet start this past spring. The summer business was not as brisk as we had hoped. Seeing how we are now into the fall schedule, we are referring most of our diners to the Tap Room. This had curbed my hours, and I have fallen a little behind on my bills. I am looking for a short-term loan with a three-year payback. I would be happy to have it attached to my mortgage as a guarantee if that would help."

"Well, Mr. Toner, I will have a meeting next Monday with the bank manager once I verify a few things on your application. Could you return next Tuesday at 11:00 a.m.?"

"Sure, that would be fine." They shook hands, and Denis departed the bank.

A few days later in the mid afternoon, Cooker strolled into Cy's and told KW to grab a bottle of red wine. "This story I wrote is gonna take a while to read to you." Cooker turned to KW after he finished reeling off the story about Pirate Pete and said, "The end." Cooker put his notepad back in his pocket and said, "That's a pretty cool story. Nicely done, if I do say so myself. You think Pirate Pete would mind if I write that into a screenplay?" He slid his glass toward the wine bottle on the table. "I'll take a refill, if you please!"

"I was going to tell you to ask him, but Pete is gone. Don't know for how long. Could be a week, a month, or until spring. He never really says good-bye. He likes to belly up to the bar often and engage with some of the local people. Other times he's just back at his favorite booth, minding his own business. It seems like too many people make him antsy, so off he goes like the wind!" KW reached over and refilled Cooker's glass.

The next day business was mildly steady, because the weather still was slightly unpleasant. KW had given the morning and lunch shifts at the bar to Donna so he could get some errands done. There were a few tasks around the restaurant he also wanted to attend to. He sat in the back booth of the restaurant, reading the *Inquirer and Mirror* and the *Worcester Telegram*. KW had considered going over to Mignosa's Market and sitting in a booth at the soda fountain there, but he knew he couldn't hide from the customers, who all seemed to know him wherever he went in town. Also Les, who leased the space, always liked to chat with KW about both of their businesses and the latest gossip, so a back booth at Cy's was about as much peace and quiet he could muster up for an hour or so unless he went home. Not a minute after he sat down, Marshmallow was up in his lap, giving out a meow and curling up. She always managed to work the crowd pretty well at Cy's and was a good attraction for customers to stop in and visit her.

Later on in the early evening, it was not too busy, just nice and steady. KW was putting some glasses away at the bar when he heard the agitated voice of a man coming from one of the back booths in the dining room area.

"I'd be better off with the old man dead," a man's voice boomed through the bar. It had a slight Spanish accent.

KW tensed up slightly as he thought to himself, *I hope this doesn't turn into some altercation.* He looked over and saw Miguel Orozco and Doug Amaral were the sources of the voices, and he relaxed and continued polishing the glasses.

Doug was a regular who hailed from Westport, Massachusetts. He had been a customer at CY's ever since KW had taken over the lease.

It was KW's first day open for business several months ago when Doug had strolled in and had Sylvia's lunch special of spaghetti and meatballs with a house salad. KW remembered Doug telling him, "Wow! If you serve food like this, you'll be packed, and you can count on me to be your best customer." Doug was a regular patron from that day forward. Over the months, KW and Doug became quite friendly in the way that barkeeps do with their customers. It's like a special bond they develop over things that are discussed and never repeated.

Doug came bearing gifts quite often when he was on the island. He usually entered Cy's with a nice bottle of red wine, a book from his father's library, or some other kind offering for KW, which he thought was very considerate. In return, KW would get him a hearty bowl of soup or something from the kitchen, which Doug also appreciated. It always brought a smile to his face. Typically Doug was at Cy's on Monday evenings by himself. It was the only bar open past 8:00 p.m. still serving any type of food.

Doug's family was in the wine importing business. Doug had worked with his uncle and father since he was fourteen years of age. As he told KW, "I never gave it much thought. The work was always there. I helped stock the shelves, making sure all the labels faced forward, dusted off some of the slower-moving selections, and swept the floors with my mother's corn husk broom. I carried cases from the back storeroom up front for the displays. I always liked to take the wood crates out back and see how high I could stack them up. I know it doesn't sound very exciting, but I made some money and it kept me busy. I remember I had to do my homework in the office after school before I was allowed to start work. A lot of the times I would have much rather been down by the water fishing and skipping stones or playing with my friends, but my father is of the Portuguese old school—commitment to the family. So that's just how it was."

Doug left the table where Miguel was and came up to the bar to pour KW a glass of a new wine that he had discovered. He had it in a bag that he brought with him. KW asked Doug, "What's up with Miguel? He seems irritated."

Doug just said, "Ah, he's just upset with his parents, and he's acting like a spoiled kid. It'll pass. I think the alcohol is helping fuel his temper a bit. I'll have him out of here in time for the next train out to Sconset."

KW always enjoyed it when Doug brought him a taste of a new wine and gave him a short background on its grapes, region, style, and so on. KW would tell Doug all the time how nice it was for a customer to wait on him for a change.

He had learned so much about wine from Doug over such a short period. It seemed almost like a trip around the globe in a wineglass. Doug would always tell him a little history about the wine and where it had come from.

He explained to KW that he began tasting wines when he was about fourteen years of age. At dinner his parents would give him a small glass of wine with a little water added to it. His father used to explain the differences of each type and style.

Over time Doug slowly began to discover his own passion for wine. By the time he was sixteen, he was educating customers about the selections, the styles, and the areas they came from around the world. People were quite amazed at this young lad for all his knowledge and insight into different wines.

"My parents seemed to recognize this quality I have for tasting and choosing wines, not only for our customers but also for selections that we stock. I love discovering affordable wines. It just seemed to get into my blood, and that's where I am today. One with the grape! Over time my family expanded their business, and now we own two shops—one in Fall River, and the other is in New Bedford. They're called Amaral's Wine and Spirits. We've built up quite the business. So far in life this stock boy isn't doing too badly for himself."

Doug often talked with KW about his family life. They spent quite a bit of time together, mostly on the quiet Mondays later on in the evening after all the other patrons had left. KW would lock the doors, and they would sit around and gab. Marshmallow would hop onto the bar and rub up against Doug while KW went into the kitchen to see what snack Sylvia had left for them. Usually she would leave a pot of minestrone soup or the soup of the day. Other times it would be pasta with red sauce and meatballs or possibly a plate of her four-cheese lasagna. Doug's favorite was her ravioli stuffed with spinach and ground pork, or sausage and peppers. Sylvia also could make a mean chicken cacciatore. She never left on Monday without putting out something for KW and Doug to enjoy. Sylvia knew that Doug would join KW after they closed up the kitchen, because almost every Tuesday when she arrived back in the kitchen there would be a note. Most of the time it was sitting under a bottle of wine that Doug would leave for her.

Dear Sylvia,
Dishes are clean and the food was delicious! I might just find a little something to bring you from the mainland next week …
God love ya!
Doug Amaral

Doug had told KW about how his father had migrated from Portugal to Westport, Massachusetts, in 1920. They arrived at a distant cousin's farm. His father also had enjoyed the sea before starting in the wine business. He was a fisherman like the vast majority of men in the coastal towns.

His mother had come over, as well, and was quite the accomplished seamstress. She had been the first one in the family to open a shop. She had a very small but efficient storefront where she set up her sewing table right in the front window. She loved to watch the people passing by. The shop was almost an overnight success. In the beginning she would bring in her cousins' tattered tablecloths and clothing along with items of her own to make the shop look busy. From the start her business grew profitable, with a steady flow of customers.

Doug's father always had enjoyed the wines of Portugal and had dreamed of opening a small wine shop.

Doug was only four years old when they had left on the ship for Boston, so his memories of his childhood in Portugal were few. Now at the age of twenty-five, he still remains fairly fluent in his native tongue. His parents did not speak much English when they arrived, and he did not speak a word of it. He still often speaks a few sentences or two in his native tongue: *Eu ch amo mam-ae* ("I love you, Mama"), *E um bom vinho e difícil de encontar* ("Good wine is hard to find"), and *E voce- estocar as prateleiras?* ("Did you stock the shelves?").

Doug's father had been looking at a small storefront in the heart of town just a few doors down from his wife's shop. The shop that was in the space was called Avery's Household Goods & Sundries. One day when Doug's father had entered the store (or, as the story goes, to purchase some tobacco), he engaged the owner in small talk. Mr. Avery was telling him that he had the shop for over twenty years. He had been an apple farmer most of his life. After he had sold the orchard, he opened up the shop and had been doing business every day since. He owned the building along with the empty spot attached to it. Doug's father asked why he never did anything with the attached storefront. Mr. Avery said, "Well, I just keep a lot of extra storage stuff in there. I guess if anyone ever wanted to rent it I could move everything over to the garage out back."

Doug's father said he might be interested in opening a small shop. Mr. Avery inquired as to what type of store he would like to open. He replied, "Wine and spirits." Mr. Amaral took out his leather pouch to pay for the tobacco, along with a few other items he had picked up.

"You giving up fishing?"

"No, not giving it up, just a little side job as a hobby, in a way."

Mr. Avery came around from behind the counter and stood by the salted cod bucket. There was momentary silence while he thought. "Let's take a look out front." He motioned for Mr. Amaral to follow him. They stood looking at the dirty window with the ratty shade that covered it from the inside. It was dusty and moldy.

Mr. Amaral said, "If I took this over, I would replace the door and reframe the windows on both sides, paint the trim, fix up the front walk with some bricks, and make a beautiful sign hanging over the entrance."

Mr. Avery again became silent as he thought. Looking at the tattered storefront and then over at his storefront, where he could see gift cards and stationery, he replied, "Well, I think we might be able to come to an agreement. I see what you're talking about. Let me talk with my wife tonight and see how she feels about it. Could you come back tomorrow around 9:00 a.m.?"

"Well, I'm not sure," Mr. Amaral replied. "I don't know if I can afford to take the whole space at this time."

Mr. Avery said, "Well, as of now all I have to do is get my sons to move everything to the garage out back. I am not taking in any revenue for the spot. So if you're going to make improvements at your own expense, I think we might be able to come to some agreement on the rent."

The next morning Mr. Amaral arrived at 8:45 a.m. Mr. Avery and his wife were both there. He took the key out of his pocket and said to Mr. Amaral, "Let's go take a venture inside. Mind you, a lot of stuff is piled in there and hasn't been touched in years. It has a fully functional bathroom, good electrical wiring, and heat. A full basement that runs the entire space of the building and above it is a one-bedroom apartment."

As they entered, Mr. Amaral looked around and saw the vision in his head. It was almost as he had dreamed about in the past. He had brought a tape measure and a pad for sketching the layout just in case this would work out. In his mind he thought, *Perfect!*

Mr. and Mrs. Avery told Doug's father to take a look around. "We'll be next door if you have any questions."

Mr. Amaral remained inside for a good thirty minutes, maneuvering around all the junk that had been piled in there for so many years. He looked at the inside of the windows for what type of light they might take in during the day, and he studied the wood floors. *Are they intact?* He looked at the rear of the storefront to see if it was ample for unloading trucks. Then he ventured down to the basement. With a little work they could enlarge the back door and make a slide to unload the boxes of liquor, beer, and wine. The basement was dry and secure. The heating system was rustic, to say the least, but with a little ingenuity it could be brought up to speed.

There was also a room off to the back left on the main floor that could easily be converted to an office, with plenty of room for a couple desks and filing cabinets. He could install a glass window so that he could view the interior of the store while seated at his desk.

Doug's father went next door and spoke with Mr. Avery and his wife. They agreed on a monthly price, and Mr. Amaral said he would like to start paying the day he opened for business. They agreed and shook hands. Three months later the first Amaral's Wine and Spirits had opened.

Spaghetti Sauce with Meatballs
    2 lb total of beef, veal, and pork, ground
    2 tsp olive oil
    1 medium white onion, chopped
    2 peeled garlic cloves, chopped
    1 tsp parsley, chopped
    1 tsp basil, chopped
    3 cans crushed tomatoes
    1 large can tomato sauce
    1 small can tomato paste
    ½ cup fresh bread crumbs
    ½ cup grated Parmesan cheese
    2 large eggs
    Salt and pepper to taste

Mix meat together, and separate half for meatballs. Cover bottom of large saucepan with olive oil. Add the meat for the sauce. After it browns, stir in onion. When onion softens, add crushed tomatoes, tomato paste, tomato sauce, and garlic. Simmer.

Sylvia's Tuscan Meatballs
Combine meat mixture, parsley, salt, pepper, Parmesan, two eggs, and bread crumbs. Mix well. Make into the meatball

size you prefer. Brown in separate pan. Use olive oil in base of pan. Add to sauce, and simmer for three hours on low heat. You may add a carrot (whole) or a pinch of sugar, if desired, to sauce.

On July 25, 1956, the Italian ocean liner the SS Andre Doria collided with the MS Stockholm in heavy fog forty-five miles south of Nantucket.

CHAPTER SEVEN

Tuesday arrived, and Denis went to Nantucket Bank for his meeting with Ms. Hutton. After they sat in her office with Mr. Sollas, the head of the mortgage department and president of the bank, things turned a little grim for Denis. "Mr. Toner," said Mr. Sollas, "we reviewed your application, and it seems to have some snags here and there."

"Well, Mr. Sollas, I hope I can correct them and answer any questions you have."

"First off, you failed to mention that you're almost four months behind on your mortgage. Not one partial payment has been made. We inquired directly with Mr. Zises, the mortgage director for Pacific National Bank. We also have a policy of a minimum of two years' current employment with the same employer, which your present job is around six months short of, and your electric and water bills are not current either."

Mr. Zises's job was to monitor all issues surrounding a mortgage that was not in good standing. "Our banks use that as a barometer for how poorly a situation might be over time. We also have heard from others that say they know you like to go off island to the racetrack in Boston and play the ponies. Am I mistaken?"

Denis knew he was not getting the loan right then and there.

"May we make a suggestion, Mr. Toner?"

"Yes, by all means," Denis replied.

"Try and get another job. We know it's the fall, but the Atheneum is looking for help. Also the Town Hall and Department of Utilities, just to name a few. See if you can work around your winter schedule at the Ocean House. Again, fall is here, and things just get quieter over the next few months."

With that said, Denis left with his paperwork under his arm and headed to Cy's for a glass of wine to drown his sorrows.

A few days later, Miguel and Doug were in the corner of the bar. "Why does he need me to go back down to Santiago to work the business?"

KW thought, *That kid is always looking for some way to get out of work.*

"I am only on Nantucket for a few months. Then we are in Miami. Then back and forth to Santiago. So who's gonna hire me? And what would I do? All I know is my family's business. I've never really done anything else out there in the working world!"

Miguel said something unintelligible to Doug, and KW wondered what exactly they were talking about. Miguel was clearly trying to keep the conversation quiet and private, but Miguel had already consumed several rum and colas.

Sometimes the loose state of conversation mixed with the influence of alcohol and made talk into gibberish, even from the best of men.

Doug, however, had not been drinking much while engaged in conversation with Miguel, who was in a state of seeming irritation.

KW shot Doug a glance and smiled. Doug rolled his eyes a bit. He knew Miguel would ramble on for a while longer. He also knew that on this day, as on other days in the past, the conversation would come to the same point. Miguel was still complaining about his father. "Papa doesn't understand me. He only thinks of the business." And as usual after a while, Miguel would become melancholy, poetic, and dreamy. "I want to live. I want to travel. I want to write a song!"

It was almost the same conversation no matter if they were out having dinner at a bar or in the kitchen at Miguel's house in Sconset. Miguel would then grow weary and become like a sleepy child. The alcohol began to take over. "I am tired. I want to rest." He would become melodramatic, as he always did.

KW knew his customers' moods like the back of his hand.

"I cannot! I will not! I will not live in the shadow of my father's life! Let's get the check and get me home."

Doug looked at Miguel and then at the clock on the wall over the bar. He had ten minutes to get him to the train, pile him in it, and shut the door, and Miguel would be on his own for the night.

At that point the door to Cy's opened and four weary travelers walked in with their bags, shaking off the damp cold. A couple of them looked a little pale. KW was sure they were coming off the boat. The seas were still running rough, and the winds had been blowing a good twenty knots for the last two days—just about enough to stop all ferries from running.

KW went over to the table and took their orders. He poured them coffee, tea, beer, and two scotches neat, along with a couple bowls of hot clam chowder and some bread. That seemed to bring them back to life.

Everyone at the bar turned to glance at the tourists and then looked away. Tourists were money. They were also inherently unwelcome sights by many of the locals, as they hated the invasion of their space. They loved the money they left behind, but they hated them for their intrusions.

This group of four was well dressed and very polite, judging from the conversation overheard at the table while serving them. It seemed that one was a doctor and the other a lawyer from Boston. They were very proper with their wives, and they were clearly of wealthy stock. They would be catered to and served well on Nantucket, but they would not be liked.

As they started to thaw out, they started berating KW with all sorts of questions. They asked what days Cy's was open and said, "The chowder was quite tasty and a good sight for sore eyes!"

They mentioned that they were staying at the Veranda House, and this was their first visit to the island. The doctor asked if they were they close to it and if it was a nice place to stay. "What kind of restaurant is the Skipper?" asked the doctor's wife.

The other gentleman asked if there were any charter boats to rent. The wives looked like they were going to turn green if they had to step foot on a boat again anytime soon. They also asked if there were any other good places to dine. They were told about the Chanticleer, the dining room at the Wauwniet Hotel, and the Moby Dick. What days were they open? Did they serve lunch and dinner? They also inquired about the lunch counter at Mignosa's Market.

KW said, "If you go to Mignosa's lunch counter, have Les make you a toasted ham and two-cheese sandwich on sourdough. He's going to reply, 'I see you've met KW.' He also mentioned that Claudette's in Sconset had the best sandwiches on the island. "It is only open from 11:30 to 2:00 p.m., but she is just about ready to close up for the season, so be advised about that."

"Is all the shopping centered on Main Street, or are there any shops in Sconset?" They seemed to be recovering nicely from the rough boat ride.

KW served the ladies more hot water for their tea and thought, *The tourist season is coming to an end pretty quickly. If the seas stay rough, it will be over until spring.*

The wives were chatting among themselves. "How will we get to the strange barn? In this weather I don't want to go traipsing all over."

They were referring to the residence at 8 Howard Street, which was the summer home and art studio that had been brought to life in the 1930s by Gertrude and Hanna Monaghan. They were Quaker sisters from Philadelphia who were considered by many of the townsfolk odd at best. KW told them that the sisters had left to go back to Philadelphia a couple weeks prior. They usually arrived in May and departed in early September.

"Oh, dear. We have missed them. Why are we here, Edward dear?" The kind doctor reminded her that they were there for the purpose of looking at a summer home to either rent or purchase. These few days were a good time for him to get away from his Boston practice.

"Sorry about the poor weather though, darling!"

The wife snapped back, "Well, the next trip, if we come back, I will not get on the boat if the seas are not calm, as it would make for a much more fashionable trip." Marshmallow sauntered up to their table and stared at the woman. She glanced down and said, "Oh my God! There is a cat roaming around!"

Marshmallow just gave out a loud meow and strolled away without a care in the world.

KW smiled to himself. *These prim and proper Bostonians lowering themselves to our island standards. How rough for them!*

Nantucket was divided by true "Nantucketers" and those who wished to be. Still, the tourists brought money to the island, and there was plenty to be had.

Everyone needed an income one way or another. There were bills to pay, so everyone coped and coexisted with the influx of tourists, whether it be in the spring, summer, or fall. The winters were their time of peace. *A funny little island with funny little people,* KW thought.

As the small group of unexpected tourists kept KW busy, he did not even notice Miguel and Doug leave the bar.

"You need to go jump on the train!" Doug told Miguel.

Miguel said, "If I had a ton of cash, I could jump on any train and go anyplace I wanted. That's all I need is a couple thousand dollars. Then I could just escape!" Miguel then said, "A nightcap at the Tap Room?"

Doug laughed. "If you miss the train, that means you're on the floor of my room with a pillow and a blanket."

"Come out to the house with me, Doug."

"Not tonight, sailor boy," replied Doug. "Now get moving!"

Miguel shrugged his shoulders, zipped up his jacket, tucked his hands in the jacket pocket, and walked away, looking over his shoulder, saying, "Lunch tomorrow one o'clock at Mignosa's? I'm buying!"

Miguel walked toward the Sconset Express, thinking that his warm bed at home sounded very inviting. He made it to the train as Marshal was closing the door. Miguel always seemed to get to the train just in the nick of time.

He wondered in his foggy state of mind how his conversation with Doug had ended. Did he get into politics, wars, or love? Or was he still just obsessing over his anger toward his father?

God only knew why KW thought this kid had a great life. They had money and lived in South America, Miami, and Nantucket. His parents seemed like wonderful people. His mother looked like an actress.

KW wondered whether Doug decided to head out on the train to Sconset and spend the night out in the beautiful house Miguel's parents owned on the Sconset bluff.

With a wealthy father like Miguel's, life couldn't be too difficult. They had a car on the island and spent the winters in the warmth of Miami with the likes of famous mobsters, actors, and entertainers like Sinatra and Capone. From what KW had heard, their home on the ocean was quite large, with a maid's quarter and a full-time grounds crew.

KW went back over to the table to see if the tourists wanted anything else for the evening. They seemed to be quite content, except the wives were not looking forward to walking the two blocks up to the Veranda House to check in. The doctor's wife commented, "It's dreadful out there. One could catch the death of cold."

As Miguel sat in the second car all by himself, he could just make out the tops of the trees blowing in the wind. The rain was off and on, not a hard downpour. The wind was not letting up, and he could see through the breaks in the clouds a full moon wasn't far off.

He thought as he drifted into a relaxed mood about his life on Nantucket. *If only this train could take me anywhere I wanted to go.* His thoughts always turned to daydreaming of leaving the island when he could. The fall storm moved and nipped at his heels.

Marshal would always ask right before he took the tickets and closed the doors if anyone had any requests to be dropped off prior to Sconset or if they needed any help loading any packages on board. He always took the time to greet all the passengers, including Miguel.

Marshal walked up to shake Miguel's hand and asked him, "Did you have a nice evening?" Miguel just shook his head and pulled his hand away. He was tipsy and didn't want to show that side of him to anyone, especially if he thought they might know his parents. Miguel just handed Marshal his ticket, almost as if he was in a daze. Marshal would always speak with the passengers briefly, sweetly, and politely if he had time, asking if they had a pleasant day or who they were visiting—just small talk, but the passengers always seemed to enjoy it.

Miguel's self-esteem was low at a point, and often he would think the other two engineers who worked the train would look down at him, except on the days when the pretty ladies were on board. Then they seemed more interested in talking with them than paying attention to Miguel.

Marshal was different. He never seemed to be anything but cordial toward Miguel. Often while waiting for the train to depart, Miguel would see Marshal sketching in a large white notepad. On several occasions, Miguel would stop and look at his work. Miguel was not much of an art fan but found himself quite intrigued by the drawings. Some were charcoal, and some were watercolors splashed onto the page. He often thought of approaching and asking if Marshal if he would sell him a few of his works to hang in his parents' home, as a gift to them, but he kept silent, thinking that Marshal might be embarrassed to have his work under such scrutiny. He probably just did this as a hobby to pass the time and didn't need a kid like Miguel to stick his nose into his private work.

Miguel thought, *Ah, I have this compartment all to myself.* Just then two older couples came scurrying up. "Oh, thank God we made it." They climbed aboard, disturbing Miguel's solitude.

He felt such an intense state of loneliness at times like these. When the train pulled out of the Nantucket Depot, he thought of some of the small train stations in which he had been. He loved them as a child. He remembered the trips he had taken with his parents on the trains to visit his cousins, aunts, and uncles in the small villages outside of bustling Santiago. Going back out to Sconset warmed his soul even on the coldest nights.

"Yes, George, I did ask Sylvia for her recipe. She wrote it down, and I will prepare it for next Sunday's dinner. I suppose the fire has gone out at the house. Gonna have to restoke it before we retire for the evening."

"Surely there will be some hot coals?" Mary spoke in distress.

"It will fire back up easily. No need to fret, my dear. I will have the rooms toasty in no time!" George said in a sweet voice.

Miguel just sat there, staring out the window almost in a mindless gaze.

The other couple moved in a little closer to each other, giving out a little chuckle as they did. They looked over at Miguel and smiled in his direction.

The two-car train didn't offer much heat. There was a small coal stove in each compartment, but it was hard to compete against the outside elements, as the insulation and the old-style windows and doors were quite drafty.

Perhaps that was why the one couple continued their small talk—to keep their minds off the fairly cold environment they were in.

It was dark on the train, but the moon offered some light when the clouds parted.

One of the men leaned over to the other couple and said, "I'm Bob, and this is my wife, Paula. We are from Chicago. We're here to visit our good friend Karen McRedmond."

The other couple replied, "George and Mary. We live here in Sconset. We love the island. Been here for ten years. We live here year-round, with a few trips off the island up to Boston and New Hampshire in the winter."

"Don't you miss the shopping in the city?" Paula asked with a smile.

"Oh, we get off island, a few trips in the spring and summer. One in September and then a couple in the wintertime when island fever sets in! We take the boat over to Hyannis, then take the Cape Codder train into Boston."

Miguel was half-asleep and half-awake. He needed solitude. Cy's had been busy, with a group of ladies chattering away right near where he sat and another loud blustering group of men on the other side of him. The small talk that was all around him on the train was enough to drive him away. Even though the train was small, he still moved to the rear and sat down on the uncomfortable wooden bench. This was still better than driving the long, mucky, rough road out to Sconset.

Miguel just closed his eyes and waited for his stop. Since he could remember, he always had loved the excitement of traveling—going somewhere new or revisiting a town. He enjoyed the sense of hustle and bustle of the big city and traveling to the different smaller train depots, with their tiny wooden structures, open windows, and old-style roofs in towns around South America.

There was something about train travel that made him feel so comfortable and relaxed. He thought back to one trip that he and his parents took to New York City. Grand Central Station was like a dream to him, with its ceilings reaching to the heavens, and the mad rush of the people going somewhere and everywhere. The brilliant sunlight that had shone through the windows from the outside was like a message from God shining down upon him.

He was only around eight years old at the time, but the memory of his father's warm hand holding him strong and tight amongst the swirl of the other travelers made him feel safe. His mother was always nearby, saying, "Miguel, stay close to your father. Don't let go of his hand!"

His mother, Victoria, was also dazzled by the size of the train station itself and overwhelmed by the enormity of the city.

Miguel still remembered feeling mesmerized by the swirl of lights, men, women, and children, all rushing with packages and bags.

The rumble of all those trains and the powerful steam engines was at the heart of the world. Being on the Sconset Express always made him ponder and recapture thoughts of his many train trips.

Somehow the magical feeling did not seem to have the effect on him lately. Tiny Nantucket, with its sparkling glass windows and chilling winds and rains, seemed to be a damper lately.

The train ride, simply put, was almost a straight line for eight miles in each direction, with the exception of Tom Nevers loop. There were always a few deer grazing alongside and a bumpy road that ran parallel to it. Nothing more.

There was nothing exciting about getting off at the Sconset stop, with the wind that could rip right off the ocean into your bones on a blustery, damp fall evening.

There were times when Miguel was confused about his life, and he couldn't deal with it any longer. Many times a wave of depression would enter his mind, and he would have an urge to walk away from it all—just go down to the ocean and walk right in and never look back.

The only way he knew how to control that urge was to keep himself warm with the burn of anger toward his father. This was one of those nights.

The four other people in the train car were sitting all bundled up, warm and snug. One couple was talking about friends and food. "That was the best brisket I've had for some time."

Miguel closed his eyes and thought of a watercolor sketch of the train as it chugged along.

It was cloudy, and there was not much to see on the dark ride home. Miguel was swaying slightly as the train moved along the dark cold tracks, and he drifted in and out of a slumber. His mind wandered anxiously around the globe in his dream space.

There was a jungle with monkeys and lions. There was a pirate ship full of gold doubloons, and a riverbank with mermaids lying along it under sparkling rainbows. He was dreaming as the train carried him home to his mother and father.

All of a sudden he felt a blast of cold air that caused him to open his eyes. He then saw Marshal opening the car doors. He was a little startled at first and felt unsettled. He wasn't quite sure where he was. He put his hand to his head. His hat was still there.

He then quickly realized he was in Sconset, and the train had stopped. The fresh cold air seemed to snap him back to reality rather quickly.

What had he been dreaming? He tried to recollect how it had ended. What did it mean, if anything at all?

Miguel rubbed his eyes and stretched his arms over his head. The dreams started to come back to him slowly. They were colorful, the sketch of a train in purples and blues trailing almost magically off to Sconset.

There had been blood on the floor of the train and some sort of bag in the corner. His father, Julio, was holding a sketch of a garden and then somehow mermaids.

Miguel let out a small yawn as he rose out of his seat. His head was now aching with epic thumps and pounds. His stomach was also churning as sourness formed in his mouth.

As he climbed off the train, he mumbled to no one in particular. This made no sense. He also wondered if Marshal knew he was drunk. When he got off, Marshal gave a polite nod his way. Maybe he was trying to save Miguel any embarrassment from tripping while getting on his way by distracting the other riders.

Probably not, Miguel thought to himself. There were four people climbing out of the first compartment, and Marshal was helping them down, saying, "Good night, and watch your step."

There was a quiet rumble of steam coming out from the front engine while the train sat idle on the tracks. The others in his compartment had already gotten off, and he could see two of them had scurried up Broadway. The other two were headed down the path to Codfish Park.

Miguel proceeded up the lane for the chilly ten-minute walk back to his family home. The cool crisp air woke up his senses and put a bounce into his step.

He mumbled as he walked, "I could use another drink." His words carried soundlessly into the night and faded into the air.

At that point there was a break in the clouds, and a full moon shined down on him. Two cats were fighting somewhere in the bushes along the road. He quickly thought of Marshmallow, and it brought a small smile to his face.

Miguel muttered to himself again, as if to an imaginary companion, "Sconset on these fall nights makes me think of witches. Witches and devils!"

As he approached his house he saw his father's light on in the study. Miguel then muttered, "Oh, no, not now. All I want to do is go to bed. I am not in the mood to deal with my father!"

His father, Julio, was waiting for him in the dimly lit entryway, as he had done numerous times in the past.

Julio was relieved when he heard the crunch of Miguel's boots on the shell path. Even with the house secured against the elements of the cold salt air, he always kept one of the front windows cracked for a little fresh air to enter the house.

Lately whenever Miguel left the house, Julio would worry endlessly that he might not come back, just walk off without a care in the world to places unknown.

Julio could sense his son's wanderlust growing every passing day—the simple hellos and good-byes, missing family lunches and dinners, and his drinking. Julio understood this to a degree, as once he was also young and full of curiosity of things to come.

But now Julio was getting older and wanted the best for his son. He wanted Miguel to begin to take life more seriously and become more responsible. All he could do was hope.

Julio was wringing his hands together, knowing that he would have almost the same conversation time and time again. "Hello, son. How was your day?" All he could do was hope that Miguel might want to join him in the study and tell him that he had done some soul searching and he thought it might be a good idea for him to return to Santiago to start taking over in his father's footsteps with the family business.

Julio was no different from any other father. He wanted his son to carry on in his family name.

Sure, his cousin Oscar was perfectly capable of running the business, but Julio had always hoped to hand the company down to his only son. Over time Julio had tried to keep Miguel involved, which he seemed to do until the past few years.

Somehow it had seemed to Julio that they just drifted further apart. Julio figured it was just a passing phase and he would grow out of it, but it seemed to just get worse.

Over the last twenty-five–plus years, the precious gems business had increased one hundredfold, and their reputation was regarded as very fine and reliable.

Oscar and Julio worked well together, but in his heart he wanted Miguel involved on a more permanent basis.

Lately Miguel's vagabond lifestyle was just zigzagging from here to there without a care. If he had money in his pocket, he would just burn through it. He seemed footloose and fancy free.

As Miguel entered the house, he felt his head pounding and a lump form in the back of his throat. He was not in any mood for a father/son confrontation, but he knew he would have to have a brief chat with Papa out of respect.

Miguel made small talk with his father and headed up to his room. Julio returned to his study and sat behind his large mahogany desk. He picked up his snifter of brandy and turned his gaze to the crackling fireplace.

He thought to himself, *Let it go*. What was the point of getting into a discussion at this time of night, knowing full well that Miguel had been drinking? Maybe he could pick a day and convince Miguel to join him at the Knotty Pine. They could have lunch and, if things were progressing well, maybe move into the comfortable chairs in front of the nice stone fireplace and enjoy a cognac, have a little bonding time, and then see where Miguel's head was in reference to returning to Santiago and working the business with Oscar.

If it wasn't in Miguel's blood, maybe he might have to let him go, let him make his own choices in life, but Julio wasn't going to give him a free ride. He would help him financially to a degree. If this was the path he chose in life, he would have to fend for himself. His mother, Victoria, might not like the choice, but the powers would be as the cards lay.

Maybe if he pulled back on the comfortable life that he had provided Miguel, he just might understand the life lesson Julio was trying desperately to teach him. Still, everything that Julio and Victoria had done had been so full of passion and energy. If Miguel wanted to choose his own way in life, it was just one's destiny, even if their dreams of passing the business along to Miguel did not fit in. It would be disheartening, but they would just have to learn to deal with it between themselves.

Victoria had been such a major part of building the business with her brilliant and creative marketing strategies over the years. Julio thought she was truly amazing. They had a very good life together and were quite successful, but like many entrepreneurs their passions had not seemed to pass down to their son.

Maybe the best choice would be to let the boy find his inner peace. Maybe it would be better to let Oscar take the reins full-time. He could adjust the profits to the task. With the business doing so well, Victoria and Oscar would never need anything ever again. With steady paychecks being deposited weekly in their bank accounts, the real estate holdings, stocks and bonds, and gold and silver, they could live a hundred lifetimes and never be poor.

Julio closed his eyes and reminisced about how they ended up on Nantucket. This always made him feel blessed and at peace.

On one of their trips that brought them to Boston several years back, they took the Cape Codder train down to Hyannis. It was a warm June day with clear skies, and summer was approaching. Victoria pestered Julio about taking the ferryboat to Nantucket. Julio had no desire to go out to the island, but Victoria had been picking up brochures about whale watching and the serenity of "The Little Grey Lady of the Sea," which got its name from the fog that settled quite often on the island situated thirty miles out at sea.

Victoria finally convinced Julio to go, and they made plans for a romantic trip, staying at the magnificent Ocean House in the heart of the town. She told Julio about the cobblestone streets, gas lanterns, quaint shops, and rose-covered cottages.

They took the three-hour ferry. It was enjoyable standing on the outside deck when they departed the Hyannis Harbor and again when they arrived at the Nantucket Port. They were greeted at the boat by a porter who accompanied them with their bags to the hotel.

They were not checked into their room for more than twenty minutes and Victoria had already unpacked and put away everything. Victoria had sent Julio to the reception to inquire about a nice place for lunch. "Well," the receptionist replied, "there's Cy's Green Coffee Pot. They have lovely home-cooked meals in a tavern setting. We have the Tap Room located on the lower floor of the hotel. Mignosa's Market on Main Street has Les's Lunch Counter. It's a simple but nice fare."

Victoria arrived and was looking at a few brochures next to the desk. She asked the lady who was wearing a name tag that read Mrs. Rea, "Where is the Chanticleer?" She was reading the simple brochure about the small inn with rose-covered trellises and a lovely restaurant.

"Oh," Mrs. Rea replied, "it's the nicest place on the island. The food is first class, and if the weather is agreeable they serve outside in their courtyard. It is a very pretty setting. To get there you must take the train out to Sconset, and it's a four-minute walk from the depot. Mind you it runs a good ten degrees cooler out in Sconset, so bring a cover-up. I would be happy to call and make a booking if you'd like, but one note, if I might add—it's pretty pricey."

Victoria said, "That would be lovely."

"I will call and see if I can arrange it with Mr. Root, the maître d'. He is a most pleasant and enjoyable person," replied Mrs. Rea.

A few minutes later Mrs. Rea (who had told Victoria to "please call me Ginny") hung up the telephone and told them where to pick up the Sconset Express. "It departs in twenty minutes and is just on lower Main Street. A ten-minute walk. They will give you directions to the Chanticleer when you get off the train. Enjoy," Ginny said with a cheerful smile.

"Just one more thing," Victoria added. "Do you have any recommendations for dinner?"

"The Point Breeze Hotel has a wonderful dining room or maybe the very quaint spot called the Woodbox. It is run by Ms. Tutine. It is one of the oldest buildings on the island," replied Ginny.

As they strolled to the depot, Julio was quite amazed at the relaxed, quiet, and quaint surroundings. The homes were decorated with freshly planted window boxes. The storefronts were beautiful but simple. The cobblestone streets were lined with beautiful trees. People were stopping and chatting with others on the sidewalks. Victoria took a deep breath in and exhaled. "I love the cool, brisk, salty air. I love this place!"

They arrived in plenty of time at the depot to purchase round-trip tickets. Victoria took a timetable and put it in her purse. Julio giggled to himself. Victoria was always picking up some sort of brochure or information packet. Back home in Miami she kept folders on all the different cities, states, and countries to which they had traveled.

The train ride out was such a pleasant experience. He was told by the conductor that the train went straight to Sconset, with no stops unless they were flagged down by someone who wanted to hop on.

It reminded Julio of the open-air trains in Chile. It almost put him in a trance-like mode, and he realized he was enjoying this trip to Nantucket much more than he expected.

Their luncheon turned out to be a very memorable experience, as well. The maître d', Mr. Root, asked if they would like to dine out in the courtyard or in the Napoleon room. Victoria opted to dine outside. The tables were all laid with red-and-white–checked linen, proper silverware, and crystal stemware.

Mr. Root—or Tracy, as he preferred to be called—brought them menus and a wine list, which was mammoth in selections. Tracy asked, "Have you dined with us in the past?"

Julio told him that it was their first visit to the island. Victoria chimed in, "And the way things are going, it won't be our last! This is a beautiful property. How long has it been run as a hotel and restaurant?"

Tracy replied, "It's been in operation since the late 1800s. A lot of our customers are theater people from New York and Boston in the summer. We have a classically trained French chef. He and his wife started working here and ended up purchasing the property twenty years ago. Over time they have brought it up to a whole new level of service and dining."

"How long have you worked here, Tracy?" Victoria asked.

"This is my tenth season. I truly enjoy my position here, and the owners are a delight to work with. The clientele we receive here are the crème de la crème. Your server today will be Rob Coles, but if I may, I would like to explain a few of our most popular dishes and inform you of the additions we are offering today to the menu. The bay scallops with spinach and truffles, finished with a light Madeira reduction, is not to be missed. I recommend sharing it as an appetizer. If you have never enjoyed Nantucket bay scallops, you're in for a real treat. Also the oven-roasted quail are raised here on a farm from the Polpis area. Our fish is delivered directly from the fishing boat to the back door of our kitchen by one our three fishermen. The chef/owner here is from Brittany and also is an avid fisherman and studies the finest recipes he can find that will match each type of fish he is preparing.

"For today's additions, we have a lovely light cream of sorrel soup. The sorrel is grown here on the property, and it's garnished with two slices of chilled lobster tail. For the entrée, we have center-cut grilled harpooned swordfish, which was brought in last night and prepared this morning. This dish is served with a sauce choron on the side, which consists of a warm hollandaise with coarse-cut tomatoes gently stirred in, accompanied by sautéed asparagus and roasted red new potatoes. Last but not least for dessert, our pastry chef has made a true apple tarte tatin, served warm with Calvados ice cream. One of those is enough to share."

Julio ordered two glasses of Veuve Clicquot champagne to begin as they perused the menu. Their server, Rob, brought out a plate of warm cheese gougeres to enjoy. Victoria and Julio raised their glasses and toasted to each other. Victoria winked at Julio, blew him a kiss, and said, "I told you that you would find this an enjoyable trip." Julio rolled his eyes at her and gave her a little smirk. This brought a fit of laughter to her, which came easily and often.

After a while Rob came over to take their order. They settled on the scallops to share as an appetizer. Julio selected the swordfish. He only had swordfish one time prior, but it was not to the standard of preparation that Tracy had explained. Victoria was still pondering her entrée selection and asked Rob to give her a few more minutes to decide. Julio picked up the wine list. He was fairly well seasoned when it came to wines, but this list was way past his realm of knowledge. He recognized many selections, but others he had never heard of. There were three different Pouilly-Fuisse, six Chablis, and all sorts of Montrachet. The list seemed endless.

Victoria selected the lobster, which consisted of butter-poached lobster meat out of the shell, served atop a light vanilla risotto and garnished with grilled fennel.

"Will you bring an extra dish for the scallops?" Rob told him that it all would be taken care of in the kitchen. "And I'll enjoy the swordfish, yes?" asked Julio.

"It's a divine dish served just about medium, not overcooked and dry."

"Excellent," replied Julio.

Rob thanked them for their order and started walking away from the table as Tracy approached. "Have you had enough time to decide on your wine, sir?"

"I think that we will go with a bottle of white. Do you have any Sancerre? I see you have an extensive selection of white Burgundy and Bordeaux."

"Yes," Tracy replied. "There are two more pages with the wines from the Loire Valley. If I might suggest, this one by Domaine Fournier is an excellent selection."

"We will take that one then. One question—I see you have Corton-Charlemagne. Which one is your preference?"

"The Bonneau du Martray is a very popular one with our guests here," Tracy replied.

"Well, we will give that a try when we come back out on another day."

Victoria said, "I remember the first time you brought a bottle of Corton from that wine shop in Miami. Oh, what a delicious treat that was."

"Well, my dear, I remember what my uncle Amalio from Chile told me when I was a teenager: 'If you're dating a woman and she orders the most expensive item on the menu, get rid of her. You will be broke your whole life, as it leads to expensive clothing and shoes in the long run.'"

Now here they were in Sconset, enjoying the good life, but still, that saying always made him chuckle to himself. They worked hard to get to where they could afford the finer things, and they both had a saying: "Life is precious. Enjoy it!"

The wine arrived in a polished silver ice bucket. Tracy presented the bottle to Julio. "The senora will try it." Victoria smiled and gave it a thumbs-up, and the lunch began.

Victoria marveled at the scallop dish. Rob brought the scallops out in a copper pot and proceeded to serve it on two bone china plates for them. They both agreed the flavors were amazing. Julio managed to get every bit of the sauce with his toasted bread.

Julio's napkin was tucked under his chin, and he looked like he was in another world, closing his eyes and savoring every bite. They were both taken to higher levels with their entrées. They were completely relaxed after finishing their entrées and lingered over the wine. Victoria said, "This place is magical. We must try to spend more time on this island to get to know it better."

As they were finishing up their dessert, the couple next to them engaged them in conversation. Don and Rita owned Mignosa's Market on Main Street in town. Victoria explained that the hotel recommended their lunch counter to them. The Mignosas said Nantucket was a wonderful place to spend the summers. They actually resided in Boston but kept their market here open from mid-April until New Year's Day. Then for the winters they headed back to Boston, where they had two other upscale grocery stores in the area.

Don and Julio seemed to hit it off right from the start. They were both cut from the same cloth of work ethics—get up early and build your business one day at a time. Don and Rita also had been to Miami in the winter months. Julio said, "If you find yourselves in the Miami area, give us a call. We would love to show you around." Victoria and Rita were engaged in their own conversation.

As they were getting ready to leave, Rita asked Victoria if they might be free the next day and could join her for lunch at the market.

"No plans as of yet," replied Victoria, so they arranged for 1:00 p.m. the next day.

Victoria and Julio strolled the quaint streets and lanes for a while after lunch in the village of Sconset. They came across several cute houses. Some were small cottages with their window planters filled with geraniums and foxgloves. They wandered past a small market and the post office. A bookstore and Claudette's sandwich shop were on the corner as they walked toward the ocean. It was a short walk around the block to Moby Dick's Bar and Restaurant. The simple sign in the menu box read "Closed for the Season. Opening Late June." They arrived back at the train depot as doors opened. The conductor named Marshal, who had engineered the train on the way out to Sconset, said, "We will be departing in ten minutes for town." He engaged them in a small conversation, telling them other facts about the island while they waited on the bench.

Early the next morning, Julio arose, while Victoria slept in. Julio headed out to find a cup of coffee and a newspaper. The hotel had a continental breakfast set up in their dining room, but Julio wanted to get out into the crisp morning air, and the clear blue sky greeted him as he exited the hotel. While he walked down the sidewalk, he remembered what Victoria had said about what a wonderful place Nantucket was. "How wonderful would it be to enjoy the summer here with family and visiting friends? We could ride bikes." Victoria giggled.

Julio gave her a look out of the corner of his eye. "Bikes?" he said.

"Maybe a nice home with a puppy running in the yard."

Julio said, "No dogs!" But he liked the other part of the scenario she was explaining.

Victoria knew what she wanted and would get it if she set her mind to do so. She wanted a house with a garden full of flowers and vegetables.

As Julio ventured over to Main Street, he caught sight of a black-and-white kitten lying in the early-morning sun in the park across from the movie theater. He thought about the quaintness of the island as he walked, and he supposed maybe Victoria wasn't too far off in her thinking. He thought, *When was the last time I strolled around a town so early in the morning, feeling so content?* Then he thought maybe a home here might be a good investment for them, but then he thought that it might be too quiet for him, too disconnected from the real world. This was nothing like Miami, but the thought lingered in his mind, and now his eyes seemed to capture more of his surroundings.

He walked up Main Street to the drugstore, sat at the counter, and ordered a coffee. He always knew that Victoria had very good instincts. He could never remember a time when she was mistaken or made an uncalculated, hasty decision. She was no fool in any business dealings into which she ventured. There was nothing open except a corner bookstore that did not seem to have any newspapers. The drugstore was next to Kendrick's Real Estate office. Inside a light was on, and a man in his forties was seated behind a desk. The sign in the window read, "Tom Kendrick Rentals and Sales," and it contained a few photos of some of their listings. One caught his eye immediately. "Delightful Sconset home with separate guest cottage or in-law suite, 1-1/2 car garage, 5 bedrooms, 4 baths, ¾ acre on the bluff overlooking the ocean, two fireplaces, a man's den, large bright kitchen. The caretaker's apartment has a wood-burning stove, one bedroom, one bath. Main home is winterized." It was listed for a pricey $64,000.

Julio sat and enjoyed his coffee. There was only one other person at the counter. When he was getting ready to leave, he asked Julio, "Would you like the newspaper? I'm done reading it."

Julio said, "Thank you very much."

"It's the *Worcester Telegram and Gazette* from a few days ago. We don't get many papers here. Our own paper, the *Inquirer and Mirror*, only comes out weekly on Thursday, and if the boats don't run we don't get any from the mainland."

"I noticed there weren't any papers at the Hub Variety Store when I ventured in a few minutes ago," Julio replied.

"The thing about our local paper is if you're not at the hub by eight in the morning on Thursday, they are usually all sold out. You would think old man Cuhna would print twice as many, but he's so set in his ways. 'Waste,' he says. 'Waste. If they don't all sell, it's money out of my pocket.' He will never change. We have all written letters stating he needs to run off at least another hundred copies but to no avail. So we do a lot of sharing. People bring them to Cy's, Mignosa's Market, here, library, the Tap Room after reading them. Of course you can get one at the newspaper office. Old man Cuhna keeps them behind the desk, like they're valuable pieces of art."

As the old man stood up, he just stared at Julio. Julio thought he was going to faint for a second. Then he reached into his pocket and said, "Congdon's the name, insurance is the game," and handed Julio a card.

He put the newspaper on the counter and walked away. Julio ordered a blueberry muffin, and the young girl behind the counter stated, "You haven't lived until you have had one of Sylvia's blueberry muffins."

Julio asked, "Who's Sylvia?"

"Oh, she runs the kitchen at Cy's Green Coffee Pot."

Julio replied, "My wife and I walked past it yesterday. Is it a good place to eat?"

"Oh yes," she said. "Sylvia is from Italy and has been cooking there forever. She's an amazing lady!"

Julio finished the paper and a second cup of coffee. He asked the Irish girl who was serving him how long she had been on Nantucket and how she ended up there. She replied that her aunt had cousins on the island, and she arrived just a fortnight ago. It was the first time she had ever been abroad. "I will be here until early September. This place is like living in a dream. I love where I live in the county of Cork. Nantucket reminds me of a small village nearby my home, but this is a wonderful change. I enjoy my job here. The people are so pleasant, and the friends I am making each and every day!" said Erin (as her name tag read).

"Do you know what time the real estate office next door opens for business?"

"It should be open soon. Mr. Kendrick arrives almost daily here, orders a coffee and a muffin to take next door."

Right then the bell hanging on the front door chimed as it opened. Erin said, "Hello, Mr. Kendrick. My new friend here was just asking what time your office opened up."

Mr. Kendrick said, "I'll be open as soon as Erin gets me my coffee and muffin. Stop on over. I will be glad to answer any questions you might have."

As Julio was getting ready to leave, a man sat down a seat away, and Julio said to himself, "Can't hurt." So he said to the stranger, "Hi, I'm finished with the newspaper. Would you like to read it?"

"I would love to," the man replied. "I have been at the Hub every day for who can remember how long, trying to get a fresh newspaper."

"Well," Julio replied, "it's not all that fresh, two days old from the mainland."

"Well, it's great." The man introduced himself. "Ken Zises. My wife and I are originally from Boston. Actually from Newton. I was in the investment business in Newton, moved down here eight years ago. I am now the president of the Pacific National Bank just a few doors up at the top of Main Street. This is a great island with great people."

Julio said, "We met the Mignosas. They're from Boston."

He was about to say they owned the market on Main Street, when Mr. Zises said, "Ah, great people, great market. They do everything 100 percent first class. My wife, Leslie, is one of their best customers. Where do you hail from?" Ken asked Julio.

Julio gave him a quick rundown on their story and then asked Ken, "Do you think Nantucket real estate is a good investment?"

"Good?" asked Ken. "It's liquid gold. Whatever you purchase, if you do it smart and treat it well, will come back tenfold, to say the least, and the reason I say treat it well is the salt air can take its toll. If it's raw land you're purchasing, it will take a slower but positive course."

With that said, Julio paid his check and went next door, thinking, *It can't hurt just asking.*

"What can I do for you?" Tom asked while standing to shake hands.

"Well, we are staying at the Ocean House. It's our first trip to the island. We went to the Chanticleer yesterday, had a wonderful lunch, loved the village and the cottages."

"Did you get to meet Tracy, the maître d' at the restaurant? He's a wonderful man."

"Yes," Julio said. "A truly delightful person. Just a quick question—is this property you have listed in the front window a Sconset home and cottage?"

"Yes, the old Vanslette place. A wonderful spot. Ken Vanslette is a personal friend of mine, known him for many years. He's decided to sell his summer home and spend more time in Ohio, where his grandkids are. He will rent for a few weeks in the summers when he comes back to the island. The house is truly in remarkably good condition. The family inherited it from their parents' parents, and they had it for the last twenty years, give or take."

"How long has it been listed, Mr. Kendrick?"

"Please, call me Tom. I put the listing together just about four weeks ago. We discussed it last fall, sitting on their deck that overlooks the ocean. He sent me all the particulars he had about the house—electrical furnace, painting, recent carpentry over the winter. I thought I would wait until May or June to list it. It also includes their island car, and around 75 percent of the furnishings will remain intact. He will come out for the wine in the cellar soon and the rest of their personal belongings."

He told Tom, "Well, let me see what my schedule is. I might like to take a look at it."

"We can take my car out anytime. And Sconset Road was repaved. Here's my card if you want to give me a call, home and office. I can be ready in fifteen minutes. Would you like to take some of the information with you?"

"No, if I do this I want to keep it as a surprise for my wife."

Julio knew he had to be at lunch with Victoria at Mignosa's Market. He figured it was one hour's drive out and back again, thirty minutes to view the property, and thirty minutes of allotted time on top of that. How could he get two hours away from Victoria without her being suspicious?

While he was thinking, he walked right past the Dreamland Movie Theater. "Perfect, afternoon matinee, starting at two thirty, a western." Victoria would not want to see it, so he could send her shopping or back to the hotel after lunch, and he could sneak off to view the house with plenty of time.

Victoria and Julio arrived at Mignosa's Market at 1:00 p.m. sharp and found Rita straightening up a front display of fresh fruit in a basket that was tipped over for an effect of them spilling out. "Hi," she said. "So glad you're here. I will be finished in a few minutes. You can stroll around or go over to the lunch counter. The booth with the reserved sign is yours."

Victoria smiled and said, "I would love to take a look around your store."

"Okay, see you in a few minutes."

Julio and Victoria were quite impressed with the store. Everything seemed to be perfect—the displays and the staff—and every aisle was spotless. Everyone with a name tag was dressed in royal-blue aprons. The counter with Laythams Fine Meats was impeccable. Behind the counter a gentleman stood in a starched white apron with a crisp white cap. Beautiful cuts of lamb, beef, liver, ground sausage, dressed chickens, quail, as well as whole stew pot packages were perfectly placed. It was a really wonderfully laid-out meat counter. They had a gift area, toys, a separate corner displaying fresh flowers, another section of imported goods, and fresh pastries. "Fresh Baked With Love," the sign read, and a lady by the name of Kathy Lee was working away. When she saw Victoria looking at the pastries, she reached over with a warm chocolate chip cookie in her hand and said, "Here, try this, just out of the oven!"

Victoria took it, and it melted in her mouth. She gave a large piece to Julio, saying, "I will never eat my lunch!"

They walked over to Les's Lunch Counter, where a young man with the name tag that read "Les" greeted them with a warm smile. "Please sit anywhere you like."

"Hi," Victoria said. "We are meeting the Mignosas for lunch. Rita said to take the reserved booth."

"Oh, okay, it's at the end there."

As they seated themselves, Victoria noticed the beautiful small flower vase on the tabletop.

Right then Rita approached, and they all sat. "Sorry, Don's off at home, sketching some plans for a new section of one of our mainland stores. He will be along shortly. When he gets an idea in his head, he won't rest until he's gotten it on paper or has a really good vision of his plan."

"Well," Victoria said, "this is a most wonderful store, so clean, fresh, brilliant displays, a really friendly and courteous staff, and wonderful chocolate chip cookies. The baker, Kathy Lee, gave me one right out of the oven."

Rita explained to Victoria, "This is the way we do things at all our stores. We lease a few sections out, such as the bakery and the meat department, also the flowers and gift cards section, which are combined into one lessee. We have strict guidelines that everything is quality or we don't use the supplier. The vendors rent space from us, and it works out really well."

"Well, the flower section is really beautiful, and the aromas from the flowers and the bakery make a person want to melt!"

"Here's a quick story," Rita started. "A couple of years ago I sat right there at that corner seat to have some lunch. Next to me was Joanne, who runs the flower and card area now. We started a conversation. I recognized her from shopping in the store, but we had never met. Well, at the end of my lunch, I thanked her for being a loyal customer. I went over, and I told Les to put that lady's lunch on my tab.

"The next morning Joanne walked in and had a beautiful vase in her hands, and it was quite striking. A beautiful mix of roses and wild flowers. So I asked her if she would like to join me for a cup of tea. I couldn't take my eyes off the arrangement she had produced. We chatted about her being from an area in Wisconsin called Williams Bay near Lake Geneva. She had heard about Nantucket but had never visited. As it turns out, friends of hers from Lake Geneva had a home here in Pocomo. They invited her out for a visit. She was here for a week and dreamed of coming back. As it happened, the same family were planning an extended trip to Europe the next summer, and they asked Joanne if she might like to come house-sit with their Labrador for six weeks. She jumped at the chance. One day while she was out walking their dog, she came upon an older semi–run-down house with a greenhouse attached and a small barn. A very small, almost unreadable sign was at the foot of the driveway, reading 'For rent or sale.'

"Joanne walked right up to the front door, met the owners, joined them for coffee, and proceeded to agree to rent the property for the next summer months. She loved the greenhouse and knew the property needed much TLC, but without hesitation she accepted the agreement. At the end of her rental contract she wrote a beautiful note to the owners and mailed it to them. She wanted to purchase the property the following spring. She now spends most of her time here while still traveling back to Wisconsin three to four times a year. She knows flowers and fixed up the greenhouse. Now she's in charge of the flower and cards concession here, and we could not be more pleased!"

Julio excused himself when he finished his large BLT sandwich, saying he was going to let them enjoy their conversation. Don looked up and said, "I am off, as well. I have some more drawings to finish."

Victoria said, "I might do some shopping."

Julio mentioned, "There is a matinee I think I might take in."

As Victoria and Rita lingered over coffee, Victoria said, "Rita, if Julio and I were to return and stay for a longer period, where would you recommend we stay that was a little more spacious? The Ocean House is a nice location, but our room is just that, a room. We would feel more comfortable in a cottage like the ones we have seen in Sconset."

Rita replied, "You should look at Tuttle's Guesthouse. It's located almost right behind the Ocean House on Center Street. You should ask for Debbie Otto. She runs the inn. They have a lovely two-bedroom cottage off to the side of their guesthouse, with a beautiful screened veranda off the back and a lovely lawn and garden with a few nice chairs and benches for enjoying your morning coffee or some peaceful afternoon reading."

"Well, that's my next stop, a stroll through town and over to see if Debbie is there at Tuttle's and possibly view the guest cottage."

Julio walked up and crossed over Main Street and was happy to see Mr. Kendrick in his office. He said, "Hello,

Tom, any chance we can go see the property? I have a quick window until around 4:00 p.m."

"Let me grab my coat," Tom replied. "My car is out back, so we can go out this door here."

"Is there a chance we don't have to go past Mignosa's Market? My wife might exit anytime now, and I don't want her to see me."

"Not a problem. We will drive out onto Union Street."

Tom Kendrick said there was also another property close by and thought it might give Julio a better perspective about the property by viewing two. The first one was in Codfish Park, a smaller two-bedroom, two-bath cottage across from the beach. It was simple but not one that caught Julio's attention much. They arrived at the other one on Baxter Road that Julio had inquired about, and the moment he stepped out of the car, Julio knew he was going to purchase it.

Julio walked around the house and the garage, as well as the cottage, which were all in excellent shape. There was no wood rot or cracks in the foundation, the roof was in good shape, the view off the back deck was superb, inside the garage there was a stairwell leading up to a loft room that was quite large, and the Chrysler wagon was covered by a couple large sheets. Julio peeked under at the car and was pleasantly surprised at its nice condition. The guest cottage was a one-bedroom and bath with an open kitchen/living room area that had a nice-sized wood-burning stove and a large attic above it, which could easily be converted into another bedroom if desired.

The main house was bright and cheerful and had beautiful wide pine floor boards, two fireplaces, and a den with a nice stone fireplace; a large airy dine-in kitchen surrounded with windows overlooking the ocean; a separate dining room; and three large bedrooms and two baths upstairs. The master had double sinks and windows that looked out to the sea. On the third floor were a large bedroom and a bath.

Julio's only concern was the furnace in the basement. It seemed to be pretty old. Tom said, "Let's see what a new one would run and if Mr. Vanslette might go fifty-fifty on the cost of replacing it."

Tom said that Pacific National Bank was very favorable for loaning money for real estate, so getting a mortgage should not be an issue. Julio said he would not need a mortgage; he would pay 100 percent the day of closing if they could get the oil burner agreement. They went back to the office, where Tom called and was able to connect directly to Mr. Vanslette. After a brief discussion about the prospective buyer and the oil burner, they agreed that Mr. Vanslette would discount the whole cost of a new oil burner, as he stated it was pretty old and the house should be, in his own words, "in move-in condition on the day of closing."

Julio returned to the hotel. It was already getting dark out, and he found Victoria reading in the library area off the main lobby, with the fireplace crackling away. She looked up and asked, "How was your western?"

"It was enjoyable. Not many people in the theater for the showing though."

Victoria also informed Julio that she had booked them dinner at the Ships Inn on Fair Street.

"The weather is looking good. I have been told tomorrow a beautiful warm day is supposed to be on the horizon. How about we book a table at the Chanticleer for our last lunch on the island? We could head out early and stroll along the bluff road. It's supposed to be a very pretty walk. Then we can enjoy lunch and come back, pack, and be ready to depart on the next morning ferry."

"That sounds wonderful, Julio. Truly wonderful."

Julio told Victoria that he was going to the room to freshen up, and he would meet her in the lobby in fifteen to twenty minutes.

He went up and called Mr. Kendrick and asked if he could get with Rita Mignosa and have a card and flowers placed on the front porch of the Sconset home. He explained their time frame for getting to the Sconset property. This was to be a surprise for Victoria.

"Sure," Tom replied. "Consider it done. Keys will be in the envelope on the porch, as well. I will also have a contract all set for you to sign tomorrow morning around 10:00 a.m. Is that a good time? Or I can drop it at the hotel."

"No, I will stop by. I don't want Victoria to get wind of this surprise."

That night they enjoyed a nice fresh cod dinner with some Linguica sausage at the Ships Inn.

The next morning Julio arose early, excited about the surprise for Victoria. He went out for his coffee, again passing by the kitten lying almost on the same spot as the day prior, meeting Erin at the drugstore counter, and getting a cranberry muffin and coffee. No newspapers were around, so he just made small talk with "Erin from Ireland," as he called her. He told her his plans to surprise Victoria while he enjoyed his coffee. She almost started crying as she said, "That's like a fairy tale."

After he finished up, he went next door to meet Mr. Kendrick and review the contract.

Tom pointed out that the contract stated Julio would be paying in full at closing. The oil burner guy, Randy, was already notified by Mr. Kendrick about the replacement of the unit and said he would have it 100 percent finished in about three weeks. Mr. Vanslette had called him, stating he had already made arrangements to pay for the installation.

Julio did a quick review, and nothing stood out from the ordinary. The only items needed were proper mailing addresses and signatures. Julio said he wanted the home to be in both names, so after the surprise he would bring Victoria to sign and they would need to stop by the bank and open a Pacific Bank account. He told Tom he met Mr. Zises over coffee already. Mr. Kendrick would also assist in getting the utilities transferred to their names, along with a few other details.

Julio went back to the hotel. Victoria was ready. "Let's take a stroll to the Brant Point Lighthouse before we take the train out to Sconset." *It's turning out to be a beautiful day in more ways than one,* Julio thought.

They stopped in the Ye Olde Curiosity Shop, Grigg's Quilts, and Benny's Kitchen Store and just glanced around. The Ye Old Shop was also owned by Benny. They discovered it had some fun toys, wood carvings, scrimshaw, and weather vanes. Benny seemed to be very knowledgeable on what he sold. Grigg's Quilts offered throws of all sizes, embroidered pillows, cashmere wraps, and Irish wool sweaters. Jeff, the owner, was extremely polite and welcomed them in and commented on the beautiful day. He informed them that they gladly shipped all of their items quickly and with insurance.

The last store they visited, Benny's Kitchen, seemed to have anything a cook could need, from wine openers to coffee presses, garlic crushers, pots, pans—you name it, they carried it. "If not, we will get it," stated Benny, who was so joyful.

Julio and Victoria started to laugh as they left the store. "This island gives you such a hometown feeling. I hope we return again and again," stated Victoria.

They headed out to buy their tickets for the train. Marshal, the conductor, remembered them and asked about their stay and when they were departing the island.

They got off the train, and Julio guided Victoria, taking her hand and glancing over at her while they walked toward the bluff road. It was a short fifteen minutes before they arrived in front of the house. Julio said, "Wow, what a sweet spot. I would love to see their view of the ocean."

As they approached the home, Victoria said, "Someone must be living here, as there are fresh flowers on the porch."

Julio guided Victoria to the porch. "Look at the flowers and the card. Must be someone's birthday."

Victoria said, "We should turn around. We don't belong on this property."

Julio smiled as he said, "The card is addressed to Victoria. Isn't that a coincidence?"

"Let's go," Victoria said, starting to turn around.

Julio said, "Not so fast." He picked up the flowers and card and said, "This is for you, my love." Victoria had a puzzled look on her face as Julio gave her the card and said, "Open it!"

"What!" Victoria let out in a high-pitched voice. "What did you do? Oh my, Julio, you have got to be kidding! Is this a joke?" she asked.

"No," Julio replied. "It's yours, all signed and sealed. Just one or two small things to clear up. We should be good to go within thirty days! Now take the keys and open the door. I am going to carry you over the threshold!" He added, "It comes with a gardener, heating guy, caretaker, and a car." And that's how the Orozco's Nantucket lifestyle began.

Grandmother Yagapucci's Meat Loaf

    2 tsp unsalted butter

    1 cup onion, finely chopped

    1 cup celery rib, finely chopped

    1 large carrot, finely chopped

    ½ cup green onion, including the greens, finely chopped

    3 cloves garlic, finely chopped

    2 tsp salt

    1 tsp ground black pepper

    2/3 cup chunked tomatoes

    1½ lb ground chuck

    1 lb spicy or sweet (or a mix of both) ground pork sausage

    1 cup fresh bread crumbs

    ½ cup fresh parsley, minced

Preheat oven to 350°F (use center rack in oven). Melt butter in large thick-bottom skillet over medium heat. Add onion, celery, carrots, green onion, and garlic. Cook uncovered for 5 minutes and then covered (stirring occasionally) for 5 more minutes or until carrots are tender. Sprinkle with salt and pepper. Add tomatoes. Cook for another 1–2 minutes. Remove from burner. Once mix is cool to the touch, add to a mixing bowl with the ground meats. Add eggs, bread crumbs, and parsley. Mix well with your hands. Place in a loaf pan (4 x 8 or 5 x 9). If desired, add Worcestershire sauce (¼ cup), or cover mixture with ketchup. Bake at 350°F for 75 minutes. Remove from oven, and let stand for 15 minutes.

Nantucket Railroad was a three-foot narrow-gauge railway that ran between Nantucket town and Siasconset. The number one engine was named Dionis after the wife of Tristram Coffin. A round-trip fare ran thirty-five cents in 1901.

CHAPTER EIGHT

The following spring Victoria had everything lined up from the notes she made after the purchase—a paint touch-up here, a new sofa there, windows washed, and air out the house. Otherwise the Vanslettes left it in impeccable condition. The tasks were at first overwhelming—maintaining the lawn and gardens, and preventing the normal winter wear and tear on an oceanfront home—but they were enjoying every minute of it. She even stopped at Benny's Kitchen Store with a list of things she was interested in purchasing. She told Benny, "Mr. Kendrick has all the particulars about the kitchen if you have any questions."

Every day they had a new adventure, strolled down a new lane, or drove down a new road. Julio looked out the bedroom window. It was nine fifteen on this Friday evening. There was a quarter moon, clear skies, and a light breeze coming off the bluff.

He had made sure the fire was out in the den, and he climbed into bed under the cool covers. His thoughts lingered over Miguel, and he hoped his focus would come back to stepping into the family business. As of the last few weeks, nothing had seemed to change. He thought of talking with Doug, Miguel's friend who he thought had a good sense of mind, to see if he might be able to figure out what Miguel's direction might be in life. As of now, Julio almost felt like he was the enemy.

The next morning Julio arose at 4:00 a.m. The skies looked clear, but it was quite cold out. Julio was fortunate enough to have met several new friends while they settled into the new house this summer. He was heading out this morning to meet Bonefish Joe, Wes Morris, and Obadiah Folger at the Tom Nevers Fishing Club.

He looked down at Victoria, bent over, gave her a kiss on her cheek, and pulled the large fluffy quilt up around her. Life was good, truly good. He then went into the kitchen and made the coffee he had set up the night prior. He enjoyed a cup, poured the rest in a thermos, and quietly slipped out of the house. There was a slight frost on the grass.

Julio had heard the weather was supposed to be mild. *A nice day for fishing,* he thought as he drove to the fish camp.

Every Saturday from late September through early December, weather permitting, Julio would meet the others at the club for coffee and doughnuts. Over coffee they would decide where their fishing jaunt would begin. If it was too windy, a pond, off shore, or on the beach, weather permitting, made their decision!

The camp was located in Tom Nevers Head, which was the southwestern part of the island. It had about forty members, and it had an area where you could post notes if you were headed out on a certain day and were looking for others to join you.

Julio usually got together with the same group of men, including Duff Myercord, a banker from New Jersey who was also one of the main principals of the Nantucket Railroad Company. Duff, so it seemed, had more money than he could ever spend, and there were plenty of scavengers vying for his time, angling to help him part with his earnings. But Duff, originally from Alabama, was a real gentleman. He was quite sharp, and no one was going to pull one over on him, no matter how smart or hard they tried. They met their match with his wits!

Duff was quite friendly with Neil Krauter, who was in the insurance business in New York and had offices in Boston, Chicago, and numerous other cities. He had ties to so many actors, wealthy families, and politicians. It was mind-boggling to hear him tell stories about all the lunches, dinners, estates, and private railroad cars he had been invited to enjoy. Duff was always kidding Neil, calling him Romeo, as Neil was, it seemed, spotted with a different lady on his arm, walking the cobblestone streets of Nantucket on his way to a dinner or a theater play. One never knew what he was up to.

Julio would tell Neil, "You're like a Latin lover, wooing all the pretty ladies."

Getting together with his fishing pals was a true delight for Julio.

Another in the fishing group was Wes Morris, a criminal attorney from the Boston area. He found that fishing was the best therapy for him to get his mind off the thieves and murderers he encountered and represented. Julio enjoyed hearing about the courtroom drama that Wes would relay to him, the real whodunits in life. In this year's big case—which got plenty of gossip and news coverage spreading throughout Boston, New York, Hartford, Providence, and even Nantucket—Wes was representing a man who allegedly had deep mob connections. Julio couldn't wait until Saturdays came around and Wes filled him in on the latest dirt and developments.

Bonefish Joe was the owner of two restaurants in town, one on Main Street and the other at the end of Old South Wharf. Both were open only in the summer months, and if you wanted to see Joe, the only place you would find him during those times was at one of the restaurants.

Joe headed to Palm Beach right around Christmas time every year. He got the name Bonefish from a friend of his who went by the name of Bubba. Joe had met him while fishing in the Keys. Bubba was also an avid bonefisher and taught Joe a lot about the sport. A few weeks later Joe caught the largest bonefish on record in the Florida Keys.

Bubba was from Mobile. He and Duff hit it off immediately. "What's the chance of two 'Bama boys being here on Nantucket?" he said to Bubba while at the bar of Joe's Main Street Restaurant. Bubba grew up in a family of sailors and sea captains. At the age of sixteen he snagged a job on a freighter and headed for Belize. After this trip, he just kept traveling, taking on different jobs, and sailing through exotic ports.

Bubba sailed into or past almost all of the Caribbean islands, carrying his guitar and his duffel, footloose and fancy free. He was never afraid to work or to have a drink with a nice island girl. Hopping ship to ship, large or small—it never mattered. He got to know many of the boats and their captains. They were always happy to see him and sort of sad to see him go.

He managed to get all the way down to South America a few times. It was rumored that he became a smuggler and made a great deal of money there. When people asked what he did for a living, he would tell them his family was in the tobacco and sugarcane business in Louisiana and Florida. Often he could be heard strumming on his guitar, singing, "The smuggling life is still for me back out on the deep blue sea. I'm a little bit older, but it's all the same. Just be careful how you run the game."

Bubba would show up on the island in his open-cockpit biplane that people said he got in a drug deal on some remote island in the Caribbean. Without a care in the world, he often spent a lot of time at one of Joe's bars with Duff, Neil, Wes, Julio, and the mysterious but always fun Hunter Laroche. Today was one of the days where out of nowhere Bubba just showed up at 5:00 a.m.

Obadiah and Scotty arrived together soon after. Scotty Whitlock was in the investment business in Boston. He would do what he referred to as the daily grind for forty hours a week. He was a major partner in the firm, but in his mind he was always on the beach, fishing on Nantucket. At times while in meetings he would nod yes and no to questions that came up during the partners' meeting, not really having a clue what they were talking about. His mind was on the beach or on a boat, casting out to get a nice fish, or heading out with his wife, Susan, for a scrumptious lunch at Cy's Green Coffee Pot. He would daydream away, almost tasting Sylvia's homemade cooking. How it made his mouth water! He ate lunch out every day in Boston. He tried to go to a new lunch spot at least once a week, but the menus were generic and the meals had no flavor. "But what Sylvia could conjure up in her kitchen came with love," he always said to his friends. To this day he would tell you he's never read the menu at Cy's after the first visit. He was hooked the minute he walked into Cy's way back when the Slimmons owned it. The aroma in the air was like he died and went to heaven. After his first meal he wandered into the kitchen to meet Sylvia, and soon after they were the best of friends. He never looked at a menu after that day. Now he just waited to be seated at a table and then headed into the kitchen with a smile and sometimes a gift for Sylvia. Many times he brought her some fresh fish he caught or a flower he picked just for her from his wife's garden, and Sylvia would whip him up a dish he couldn't have dreamed about.

When he heard that the Slimmons were selling the bar, he almost had a heart attack. He met KW, the new prospective owner, and pleaded with him to keep Sylvia, even offering to give her a raise out of his own pocket if she stayed.

Obadiah Folger was another member of the group. He was a town selectman and also a descendant of original settlers. He was usually the first to arrive at the fishing camp, letting himself inside and striking a match to the fireplace and the wood-burning stove located in the center of the fishing club barn. He always brought some food to snack on and put what was needed in the icebox, along with a bottle of Veuve Clicquot champagne, which was a standard weekly ritual for him. They all brought something to share. Among the favorites were some wine, spirits, and cigars for after the morning of fishing. And there were plenty of supplies for them to enjoy an afternoon of storytelling, frying their catch, playing cards, or reading by the fireplace. This was the life at the Tom Nevers Fishing Club.

Everyone seemed to arrive around the same time. Neil arrived second to last—that always seemed to be the case. His reply was "I live on the total opposite side of this island. It takes me a while."

With that Duff chimed in, "And of course there was no lady involved in making it a late night, was there, Neil?" And right on their heels in walked Bubba, all full of firecracker energy, guitar in hand. Joe asked, "When did you get in, last night? You got that cockpit still open? If so, you must be frozen to death."

"Nah, I was in Boston, so I took the train down yesterday, strolled around Hyannis for a while, took the late ferry over. Stayed at Hunter's place in Sconset, borrowed his car, and here I am."

"Had I known, I could have brought you in," Julio said.

Julio laid out the walnut bread Victoria had made the night before. Duff and Joe brought more coffee and doughnuts. With the sugar and caffeine starting to kick in, Bubba hollered, "Who's ready to catch a whale?"

Wes let out a great laugh and said, "Only you, Bubba. Only you!" He grabbed two doughnuts and said, 'Where we headed? I'm ready to go!"

The men all decided that they would head out to the jetties They had heard reports that there were some good-sized stripers running earlier in the week. They stood, clapped Bubba on the shoulder, and shook his hand. It was always a good day when Bubba joined them.

After a few hours of fishing, they packed it up and headed back to the camp, shed off their wet fishing gear, stoked the fires, and changed into some dry clothes. Earlier in the year, Randy, the oil burner guy, had installed a unit that kicked off pretty good heat, and he installed a great shower with hot water that never seemed to end—a true welcome back when he was chilled and damp from three to four hours of fishing in cold temperatures.

The table was set with platters of sliced meats, cheeses, and breads when they arrived. Krebs was there, putting together a nice lunch, and ready to fillet the fish, if they caught any.

Krebs was a good friend of Bubba. He met him a few years back with Joe. Krebs was more of a pond fisherman, not an early riser, but he knew a lot about the sport and meshed well with all of the club members.

He would keep a small bottle of blackberry brandy in his pocket. He said it was "always good for what ails ya or to keep you warm and toasty!" He always looked forward to these Saturday-afternoon getaways.

Obadiah was feeling a little anxious today. He wanted to get a few moments alone with Julio. He really liked Julio's business plan and the history of the progression of the business. He wanted to see if Julio might be interested in having a small investor. The mystery of South America and the profit margin that Julio had discussed with him over a few past lunches together had him intrigued.

Obadiah wanted to invest twenty-five or even fifty grand with him if he agreed. He did some research on the precious gems and metals business by calling a business friend in New York, who told him it was exploding and prices were rising rapidly. During the day he managed some small talk with Julio, but there was always somebody around and the time never seemed right to broach the subject.

At one point Bubba let out a "Whoa, boy! I got one! She's a beauty. I can tell by the way my line is dragging."

"You go there, sailor boy!" Neil yelled out. "You get them, Bubba!"

Obadiah used the opportunity to say, "Julio, can we meet sometime soon to talk?"

"Let's talk here, my friend."

"No, not at this time. I want to keep it personal."

"Is everything well with you?" Julio felt concerned. *What could be wrong?* he thought.

Obadiah hesitated. He wanted to keep this investment idea a private matter and did not wish for the others to overhear his thoughts on approaching Julio.

"Julio, it's a good thing. This is not the time or place to discuss my idea. Can we meet for afternoon drinks or dinner at the Ocean House Monday?"

"Surely, yes. Should I bring Victoria?"

"Best that you don't—not yet, at least. Let me see what you think of my proposal first." He gave a wink and a smile.

"Oh, it's about money or business, is it?"

"Isn't it always?"

They both turned to look at Bubba, who was laughing and trying to coax the large fish onto the shore.

They finished up the morning, catching eight stripers and a few smaller rock bass, along with some blues that they had tossed back.

Back at the camp the warm surroundings felt good. The new shower was a true delight for Julio, the fireplace crackling and the wood-burning stove toasty. Krebs quickly made easy work out of filleting the fish. The table was laid out with meats, cheeses, crackers, bread, and condiments, and Krebs had his glass of red wine by his side. Neil, Duff, Wes, Bubba, and Joe were engrossed in a card game over by the potbellied stove telling stories as usaul. Bubba was telling the story about him and Neil fishing on the beach by Eel Point. Bubba kept laughing while he said, "Do you remember that gusty, cold windy day at the beach? When I asked if that shack up there was all yours?" Now Neil was chuckling. "Yeah I remember your face when I took you up to my shack. All 9000 square feet of it. It's only got 12 bedroom, 14 bathrooms and a 4000 square foot cottage. It sits on a measly 42 acres. Aah, life is good my man. Life is good." The champagne glasses were set out for the traditional toast with the Clicquot Obadiah had brought.

Obadiah finalized his plans quietly with Julio, explaining that he had a substantial amount of cash on hand and he wanted to talk about the mine that Julio had discussed a few weeks back. Obadiah and Julio agreed to meet at around three on Monday.

Bubba was strumming on his guitar, singing, "It's all good in Tom Nevers at the fishing club with the striped bass gang."

Maria Mitchell was born on Nantucket from Quaker ancestry and became a famous astronomer.

CHAPTER NINE

Monday morning arrived crisp and clear. Victoria took the train into town. She didn't mind driving, but the train was just easier. She always feared hitting a deer when on Sconset Road in the spring and fall.

She enjoyed the peaceful train ride and looking at the scenery, which mainly was miles and miles of forestland. She was under some stress lately, because Julio was trying to get Miguel to commit more to the family business, which she agreed with, but it seemed to make Miguel more distant.

Back at the house Miguel was in the kitchen, and Julio made idle chat with him. Miguel was not one for much conversation lately. Julio said, "I really would like for you to go back to Santiago and spend the winter working with Oscar. Taking an interest in the family business, in a few years you would have great responsibilities. Make a name for yourself. In the summers you could still come to Nantucket."

Miguel did not look up. He just kept buttering his toast. "Nothing you can do will make me go back to Santiago. I like it here in the States. I will go to Miami, but that's as far south as I am traveling. Or maybe I will just travel on my own, see the country."

Julio looked in disbelief. "Without working for the family company, what will you do for an income? Where will you live? As of now, you have never had to pay for housing or anything really. You have no savings except what we have given you, no car, actually, nothing to call your own."

Miguel stormed out of the kitchen and said, "I can take care of myself!"

Julio let him go. It was now 2:00 p.m., and he had to meet Obadiah. As he drove down Sconset Road, he couldn't help thinking about how badly his conversation with Miguel had ended.

"Obadiah, so nice to see you. Shall we sit over by the fire, where it is a little more private?"

"Julio, nice to see you, as well. Yes, I would prefer the conversation stay between the two of us."

As they sat, Julio started to explain about how his grandfather had started his business. "We have been in business over seventy years in Santiago. We have a triple-A rating for credit with Banco de Santiago, where we have had a relationship since the day my grandfather set up shop. We are now in the process of looking at another mine located in Brazil that has been abandoned."

"Yes, Julio, that is the one I am interested in investing in."

"My cousin Oscar had contacted the owner and inquired about selling it to us. It covers all mineral rights in the sale along with one 130 hectares of land. The mine is well constructed but needs reinforcing. Oscar was given an inspection okayed by the current owner, a German, Baron Hans Bokelman.

"Oscar went into the mines on eight different inspections with our foreman and two other gemologists that we employ. This is our usual procedure when we are considering a property for either leasing or purchasing for exploration. The first four trips revealed little or poor results. Then on the fifth trip one of the gemologists, Mr. Caselli, chiseled for about two feet into a discontinued side shaft and thought he saw a vein of Paraiba. It is an extremely valuable and rare gemstone—an aqua blue with a hint of green in color, never to be matched in its brilliance. It's like finding a flawless or extremely clear diamond. Very, very rare.

"So on the substantial three other explorations, Mr. Caselli felt that this mine was a good option. So we approached the baron, who is no fool. He's very keen and suave and a good businessman. It is good that we are dealing with a serious person and not some flake who will try and make our purchase null and void if we make a discovery."

Obadiah seemed truly interested. "I told him the Banco de Santiago would loan us the funds to purchase without a hitch, and that's what we are considering. We were in talks back in February with the baron. We did not want to seem too anxious, and we felt that the mine was not going to be sold anytime soon. If we acted too quick, he might hold strong on the price. We just remained quiet. The baron did contact us a few weeks later, asking if we were interested. Oscar replied, via telegram, that we were researching in Argentina and we would get in touch if we were inclined to move forward. Now that it's been almost nine months, we are now looking to move forward. But then again, we are an upstanding, honest company, and we don't want to have the baron feel cheated if we were to discover a good streak of Paraiba, as a few good gems could almost cover the cost of the whole purchase. So we are setting up to see if the baron might want to sell it to us at even more of a discounted rate and in return receive 15 percent of any monies we receive from the mine if he discounts the mine by 40 percent of the sale price. We did not mention the possibility of Paraiba being discovered. If so, he would never sell.

"There are two good things this type of agreement brings forth. First is if he refuses and we hit it big, he cannot come back at us, saying we cheated him out of his mineral rights. Second, if he accepts the 15 percent of monies from our findings, we get the mine at a huge discount and he gets some royalties."

"What do you think the answer is?" asked Obadiah.

"Well, the baron is wealthy. We did a background check on him, as we are sure he did with us. He's from Heidelberg, where he was in the shipping business—the third largest in Germany. So we think he will take the lower sale price and keep his option open, as he is not in need of money, and the mine is useless to him as of now.

Obadiah sat quiet for a moment. Then he said, "I like your approach to this and your keen business sense. With the bank involved, you would have to pay interest on the loan. If I were to be involved, we could draw up a simple gentleman's agreement, where I would receive a percentage of the mine's royalties and the option to pull out at any time, with a cash reimbursement agreement on what we both thought was a fair deal. I would like to bring you the fifty thousand dollars in Sconset this week. I will call you with the details."

With that they stood and shook hands, and Obadiah departed.

Miguel headed to Cy's Green Coffee Pot and saw Cooker reading a book at the bar. He explained to Cooker what had transpired between him and his father. They moved to a booth in the back of the restaurant. Hoody, who was tending bar, shook his head at Cooker, as if implying, "What an idiot this kid is!"

"Hey, Hoody, can I get another glass of wine?" Denis Toner asked.

"Coming right up."

"Where's KW today?"

"He took the rest of the day off. He was going to meet Turrentine down at the Lobster Pound. He and Steve are gonna chow down on some lobsters that are coming fresh off the boat today. You know they sold out of lobster the last two days? There was a big wedding group yesterday. They took the whole place, and the day before it was the VFW guys and their wives for a private clambake on the patio. So people who came out to the island and had their hearts set on a lobster boil at the pound were not happy campers. We had several in here talking about the place being closed for private parties. They asked if we served lobsters, and I had to tell them we only offer them on Thursdays. I gave them the whole spiel—served either baked, stuffed, or simply boiled. I also told them if you're not here by 5:00 p.m. you're gonna be out of luck. We've been serving them with Sylvia's maple syrup corn hush puppies, boiled corn, coleslaw, and the thick cut of the slowly cooked smoked bacon. Never fails, we are sold out totally by 6:00 p.m. We had a wedding group the night before. They took over the place. We gave them the back part of the restaurant for cocktails and a buffet table. Nice group, and they drank like fishes! You know how it is when someone else is picking up the tab?"

"How well I do," replied Denis. "Hey, Hoody, you think I could have you hold my tab for a few days? I got a couple bills I want to clear up, and it's been kinda slow at the hotel this week."

"I am sure that's gonna be fine with KW. I'll leave a note with it on his desk in the office."

The booths at Cy's were high backed and offered diners some privacy. Miguel told Cooker, "I'm going to find a way to get some fat cash and get to Florida. Find a place of my own. Or maybe I'll take a slow boat to Europe or a train across the country."

Cooker mused, "Maybe I'll join you. A few months in the sun and a tan would do me some good for acting jobs. A nice color on my skin might help me in auditions. Or we could head off to Europe, find some French broads." He chuckled.

A few days later Cooker found Miguel at the bar and said, "Hey, buddy, how are things going with you and the old man?"

"Nothing's changed. I've got to get out of here. Let's go sit in a booth. I'm getting hungry. I want some chicken potpie."

As they sat at the table Miguel said, "When are you going back to New York? Maybe I'll scrape some dough together and go with you. I've got some cash stashed—not a lot but enough for a while. Maybe you can get me a job on one of the sets? I'm open for any type of work. I've got to get my life together."

The potpie arrived. Cooker grabbed the small bread plate, scooped up a bit of the potpie, reached for the butter, and slathered a piece of bread.

Miguel said, "Hungry there, Cooker?"

When Cooker got up to leave, Miguel remained behind in the booth to think for a while. He could hear the conversation between two male voices in a hushed whisper—something about the train and heading out to

Sconset in a few days. *Sounds like someone with a bunch of cash is going to be on it,* thought Miguel.

"For some cash in hand. Deal?"

The other guy said, "Look, all you have to do is pick me up at the four-mile marker on the night it goes down. I should have the information on the day and exact time, but I'm pretty sure it'll be the 7:00 p.m. ride out to Sconset. I will get you the hundred bucks. All you have to do is back your truck up and park it out of sight."

"Now, if I get the plans straight, I am going to have to find a way to stop the train en route?"

"I might need you to cut a tree across the track after the prior run into town from Sconset."

"Make it 150 and I will drive the truck out and get the tree cut. I'll stop that train dead in its tracks and hurry down the road back to my truck. I can be all set and waiting, engine running. You can be in and out in a jiffy. You would have to be quick like a jackrabbit, grab the money, and go, all covered up in the dark shadows. No one will recognize you. The element of surprise, my dear Holmes."

"Holmes. I'll give you a Holmes! What do you think you are, a detective? I'll have to get the final plan quickly, find the spot close to the four-mile marker, the train goes past it, about one minute, and whammo! There's the downed tree. Jump on, jump off."

"What if the guy has the money in his pocket?"

"I will find it. Don't you worry about that. You just have the tree down, and I will do the rest."

"How much cash is there to be had?"

"About a grand, possibly."

As Miguel overheard this, he was planning his own scenario.

"The only deal is you gotta pay me up front, because If you don't score the money then I'm out of luck. I am not doing all this stuff for you."

"Well, I can arrange that, but after you drop me in town we are done! Don't try and be chummy with me when this is all over. This is just a business deal—no more, no less. You get what we have discussed. Don't try and jack me up for more money! You drop me in town, and that's it. We are finished."

"When and if it happens, right after the heist, I am going to lay low and get off this friggin island."

Miguel didn't overhear any names, many details, or the exact night, but he understood it would be soon. *The early evening train and cash.* His mind started to wander. *Cash. Escape. Travel. Freedom.*

He quietly paid his bill and slipped out, not wanting to be seen by the men in the next booth—just in case. His mind started racing again as he walked slowly to the train. He did not want to go home. Deep in thought, he said to himself, "Something has to give." He had to make a move, sooner rather than later. He would have to take the train every night at 7:00 p.m. and see who was carrying what. "What does a container of money look like? How am I gonna do this? Grab it and jump off the train? Beat this other guy at his own game? What if the guy has the money in a jacket pocket and I can't spot it? How much are they talking about? How much cash could I score? Must be a good amount if it this guy is planning it."

A grand would last Miguel quite a long time, and he would add it to the money he already had stashed away. "A couple grand? Maybe more?"

The next night Miguel went to the station a little before seven o'clock. He stood off to the side near the benches, which was a small distance away from the depot. Nobody seemed to be paying attention to him. He was trying his best not to look suspicious. He had his knife in the right front pocket of his coat, his collar was up, and his hat was scrunched down over his brow. He waited to be the last person boarding. He sat on the bench and watched the people who were getting ready to board. No one stood out. "Could it possibly be a woman?" There were two ladies carrying a few shopping bags, a couple with a small child, two other guys who were pretty well oiled with liquor from an afternoon in town, and that was it.

When it was time to board, the conductor, Jim Jaksic, a guy he recognized but never spoke with, asked, "Getting on, son?"

"No, just waiting to meet some friends. Thanks." Miguel strolled away, thinking, *Again tomorrow night, same time.*

The next day Miguel had been drinking in the late afternoon at the Tap Room. He was nervous, going over and over in his mind how this grab-and-go could work. He meandered down to Cy's and had two shots of tequila and two quick beers before heading for the depot.

He felt woozy as he stood under a tree across the street. He had a good view of the people boarding the train. He was there in plenty of time, so again he could spot the potential target. He watched as a few stragglers showed up and waited to board. There was a girl he recognized from the soda fountain at the drugstore, an older guy who he knew from the bars in town who lived in Tom Nevers, a younger boy and girl around sixteen years old who looked like brother and sister, and Neil Krauter, who he knew from Cy's, with a pretty lady on his arm. Everyone entered the front compartment, possibly to keep warm. Miguel did not see anyone else boarding.

As the time approached to depart, Miguel saw Obadiah Folger moving at a pretty good pace, heading for the train, briefcase in hand. He did not know the man personally but had seen him around at different times. People always said, "There's old man Folger. He owns half of Main Street, cheap bastard." Hoody used to say, "He's got tons of money and is going to die with it. Lousy tipper, that gruff old man. Thinks he's better than most."

Miguel boarded and sat in the same compartment, the second car of the train. It turned out it was just him and old man Folger in their compartment. The sky was blanketed with clouds and made for a dark night. The only light on was the one that shone off the front of the train onto the tracks. Folger kept the briefcase tightly in his hands, on his lap. It was a cold and breezy evening, and the old man was wearing cloth, not leather, gloves.

That should make it easier to grab that out of his hands, thought Miguel.

Miguel's plan was simple. When the train slowed and came to a stop, if the tree was down, he'd stand up like he was concerned and move closer to the old man. Right when it stopped, the conductor would be trying to figure out what exactly was going on. Miguel would grab the case and jump out the back door and run like the wind.

Miguel's palms were beginning to sweat, and his heart was pounding. The ride seemed to take forever. It seemed like the longest four miles of his life. But soon after departing the depot, Miguel started to feel tired as the alcohol and damp cold seeped into his bones. The train swayed side to side, and he felt his eyes starting to get heavy. With all the nervous energy and the other factors weighing in, he slowly but reluctantly dozed off.

Then it happened. The brakes came on suddenly and made a small screech, and the train came to a jarring stop, enough to shake old man Folger from a peaceful ride to a more upright seated position.

It was quite dark when Miguel was jolted awake. At first he was lost in a daze. He was waiting for his eyes to adjust to the darkness. He realized quickly that he must have fallen asleep. Miguel was still trying to clear the cobwebs out of his head. Was he awake, or was he dreaming? He sat on the hardwood bench. There was some sort of commotion going on almost directly in front of him. He finally started to regain his senses. *The tree must be downed.* The front door of the compartment was open, and old man Folger was sitting there. He could just make out his silhouette. He also seemed to be asleep, wheezing quietly, as if he was snoring. Miguel moved toward old man Folger. He heard voices coming from outside the train. He had to move quickly. Within a few moments he was off the train and disappearing into the woods.

"What's going on?" a lady asked.

"Most likely just another deer," a man replied to her.

"Yes, probably."

The conductor looked puzzled as he got off the train, seeing the fallen tree across the tracks.

"Look at that," George Williams said, exiting the train, his wife, Mary, following him. "Strange," he said. "There's no wind blowing."

The conductor walked up to the tree, and George followed. "Looks like it's been cut down, Jim," he said to the conductor. "That's strange. Well, whatever the cause is, we still need a few men to pull the tree off the tracks."

"I think we have enough manpower here to move it."

As they all gathered around, everyone knew it wasn't the wind that caused the fallen tree.

"Maybe rotten roots?" one woman mused to another.

The base of the tree was in the thick brush, so they couldn't be sure in the dark of the night. The conductor grabbed a lamp from the engine room and tried to get to the base, but the brush was too thick. The conductor figured it was best to locate the cause in the morning.

George Williams was too curious. This freak accident did not sit well with him. He took the lamp, forged through the brush, and hollered, "It's not a natural fall. It's been chopped at the base. It has been deliberately cut down!"

Shelia Egan was on the train, looking in disbelief. Turning up her coat collar in the mid island night, she said, "Who would do such a dangerous thing? Why? Had this tree landed on the train, someone could have been injured or, possibly worse, killed!"

Neil was sitting there very contently, seemingly without a care in the world, with his arm snuggly around his date.

The men gathered to see if they could lift the tree off the tracks. Obadiah Folger sat in the second compartment, alone in his seat, not moving. At first no one even thought about the two passengers in the last compartment, even though the door was open. The people would soon discover something was wrong with the older frail man in the rear compartment.

One of the men walked back to see If there was any more manpower to help lift the tree off the tracks and noticed Obadiah Folger slouched in his seat. His assailant had slipped off the train and walked into the darkness of the woods. No one heard or saw a thing.

Only two people knew that Obadiah was carrying a briefcase full of money. Miguel was one, and the other mysterious person was no longer to be seen near the train. The attackers were long gone with the briefcase by the time they discovered Obadiah. It was too late. He was deceased.

The farmer who discovered Obadiah yelled in a panic, "Help, help me, Lord! I think this man has had a heart attack. He's not breathing. Come quick. We need a doctor. Now! Sir, sir, can you hear me?"

There wasn't any response. Obadiah did not make a sound. His eyes were closed, and there was no breath coming from his lifeless body.

The conductor was the first to enter as the farmer cried for help, followed quickly by George Williams. They also checked Obadiah for life but found none. The farmer's wife entered and laid her shawl over Obadiah's shoulders as the others stood outside the train. George Williams thought to himself, *A death and a tree cut down? What does it mean?*

Neil overheard the commotion and rolled his eyes, wondering what was happening, never removing his arm that was wrapped around his date.

The farmer's wife held Obadiah's cold hands in her warm ones and, with the others who had now gathered outside the train's window, recited the Lord's Prayer.

As the farmer's wife finished, she laid Obadiah's hand on his lap. Then she noticed what looked like blood. At first it was concealed under his heavy wool coat. "Blood!" she shrieked. It was hard to see at first in the darkness and was only illuminated by the conductor's lamp. "Why all the blood? Oh my God," she wailed.

The conductor and the farmer escorted her off the train. "There's been a murder on this train!" They quickly inspected Obadiah. "He's been plunged with a knife into his lungs! This wasn't a heart attack!"

With the discovery they decided the train had to remain where it was. It was now a crime scene. George Williams walked through the woods a short distance to Sconset Road. After about twenty minutes a car came by. George flagged it down and explained the situation. The car was headed to Sconset. The driver turned around, as George instructed him. "Take me directly to the constable's home." It was late in the evening, and George wanted to get the constable to the scene quickly to secure it.

Constable Cosmo called Deputy Donato at home and had him meet them at the rotary with Mr. Williams. They decided that it would be best if they drove to the murder scene together.

They walked through the woods to the train and found Obadiah just as he had died, except with the added shawl the farmer's wife had placed on his shoulders.

The rest of the riders were all in the front compartment, trying to keep warm. "Does anyone remember seeing any other passengers in the last compartment?"

"Don't really reckon," one said to another.

The young girl said, "I think someone got on at the last moment, but I am not too sure."

"I did see Obadiah getting on right before we departed. He was carrying a briefcase, but that's all I remember," Shelia Egan mentioned.

"Briefcase? That's funny. There's no briefcase with him now. Are you sure, Shelia?"

"I think so. I wasn't really paying attention. I only noticed him because he was at a bank meeting with me a few days ago. He always carries a briefcase, it seems. Maybe I just thought he had one with him? No! Now that I think of it, it's clear in my mind. He did have a briefcase with him."

As Constable Cosmo examined the body, Jim Jaksic explained to him and the deputy that they had not disturbed the body. He went through the motions that followed the discovery with the prayer and who had entered the compartment since then.

"This doesn't make any sense!" said Shelia Egan. "He was a gentle soul and didn't have any enemies."

The constable got down on his knees for a closer view of the body. He then reached into Obadiah's pockets and pulled out his wallet. "Doesn't seem to be a robbery, as his wallet is intact with sixty-five dollars cash inside of it."

"So he was killed? For what reason?" asked the deputy.

"I'm not sure," Constable Cosmo replied with a puzzled look on his face. "This is the first murder I have ever come across in my last eighteen years here on the force."

He knew Obadiah from the Rotary Club, the VFW Hall get-togethers, and the bank meetings where he was on the board.

"Now why would a person want to murder Obadiah? Was the murderer on the train? Or did they cut the tree and enter after the train stopped?"

Deputy Donato interviewed the riders, but no one could recall seeing any suspicious activity.

Jim Jaksic mentioned that Shelia Egan was pretty sure Obadiah was carrying a briefcase with him, and it was no place to be found. Constable Cosmo looked under all the seats, thinking he might have dropped it when the train came to such an abrupt halt.

At the end of his examination, the constable, using his flashlight, found something under Obadiah's seat. It was a small tear of fabric and a lone cuff link—yellow, with an older heavyset lady in the center with the initials VCP.

He wondered if this had any bearing on the case. He placed the torn material and the cuff link into his pocket, not mentioning this to anyone except his deputy. Then he told him, "Keep this quiet for now. It might be a clue."

He was thinking, *A murdered man, a missing briefcase, a cuff link, and a piece of what resembles a torn shirt. Was this a robbery gone bad after all?* He couldn't be sure because of the passengers' claims of not seeing anything when it was all in such close proximity. Was there or was there not a briefcase missing?

He then thought about the scenario again. *Maybe the killer chopped down the tree, hid in the woods until the train stopped, opened the door quickly, and in the darkness grabbed the briefcase. Maybe Obadiah gave a struggle, grabbed at his assailant, and tore his shirt in the struggle prior to being stabbed.*

At this point another two cars had stopped on Sconset Road when they saw the constable's car with its lights on. They walked over to the train. The constable asked them if they had seen any other cars on the road or any persons walking along. "None," they both replied.

With that Neil asked one of the drivers, as if nothing had happened, "Do you think we could grab a ride out to Sconset?"

It was cold. Constable Cosmo and Deputy Donato did a short interview with each passenger, taking notes. They removed Obadiah's body and placed him in the waiting ambulance. Everybody gathered together and removed the tree with much ease off the tracks so they could get out of the cold and into their homes.

The very next day Constable Cosmo asked Karen, his secretary, "Karen, could you please, first off, get Captain Andresen of the Steamship Authority on the phone?"

"Right away," she replied and went to her desk. She yelled back, "Cosmo, I have Captain Andresen on the line."

"Hello Spider," Cosmo said into the receiver. "How are things these days?"

"All is well. Not much changes except the weather and the tides."

"The reason for my call is we had an incident on the train last night, and a person whom we have some questions for might take a trip. So I will give you his description. If you see him, don't acknowledge him. Just get in touch with me at my office. If I am out, let the dispatcher know that I've instructed you to have them radio me ASAP, and just stall the shove-off of the boat. Cite an oil gauge problem or something. Also, I would like you to do a very casual walk through the boat decks prior to casting off. If you think you have spotted someone who fits the description, just be very casual. Don't alarm the person."

Next he had Karen call out to the airport and put him in touch with Tim Lonnergan, who was in charge of the Nantucket Airport Authority. "Hey, Tim, how are things?" asked the constable. "And how's the wife? I am glad I caught you at work. We really need to get together sooner rather than later for dinner." He then relayed the same message that he had to Captain Andresen.

Next he had Karen telephone the passengers on the train who left phone numbers. Karen called all of them to set up interviews.

Cosmo took a stroll down to the harbor master's office that was run by a retired navy commander, Ted Hudgins, who loved to think about the thrill and excitement of smugglers running off the waters of Nantucket and Cape Cod. He was always telling people of fast chases and mystery boats off the coast. Everyone thought he never truly got the war out from under his belt. You could often hear someone yell up to his office window day or night, "Any smugglers running under the darkness of night, Commander?" Then they would start laughing. Many thought his stories were quite amusing. Lots of people enjoyed being at cocktail parties and listening to all of the stories he loved to tell.

Cosmo more or less relayed the same request to Commander Hudgins about keeping an eye out. Commander Hudgins was so excited at this real piece of Coast Guard style of investigation that he saluted the constable and said, "Aye aye, Chief!" The constable also had asked each of the department heads to keep this search semi-quiet so that a lot of false leads would not turn up.

One thing he knew was that the commander was so hungry for some excitement that he was sure he was going to be telling everybody and anybody who would listen to him that he was on a covert mission and wouldn't be able to divulge anything about it.

Cosmo chuckled as he walked away. He wouldn't be surprised to see the commander driving his old army jeep up Main Street later on in the day, with his flashing Civil Defense light attached to it. The three flags, two in front on each side of the bumper and one directly center off the back hatch: the US flag, the Nantucket Island flag, and a Navy flag. "Whatever did it mean on an army vehicle?" Cosmo never understood. He'd be dressed in his full navy whites and his famous sword that he told everybody within earshot that he had taken off a prisoner in the Pacific many years ago.

Karen was lucky enough to have gotten in touch with all of the train passenger witnesses. Neil Krauter made it seem like this was a waste of time, stating that he had not seen anything, nor had his date. Karen had given each of them a time frame in which the constable would like them to come in and asked if each one would be able to stop down at the station and provide a handwritten statement of the night's events, from the time they boarded or even a few minutes prior, until he had arrived on the scene.

Within two days' time they had all come in and accounted to the constable and Deputy Donato the events that had transpired that evening. They uncovered an interesting bit of information. The young girl, Sonya, recalled seeing Miguel Orozco board the train at the last minute. "He got into the same compartment that the man Mr. Folger was in."

"Are you sure?" asked Deputy Donato.

"Yes." she replied.

"Why did you not mention it two nights ago?"

"I was a little shaken up. I have never seen a dead person, not even at a funeral. I guess I was a little taken back and not thinking straight."

"What about you?" the constable asked as he pointed to her brother.

"I didn't see anyone get on. Not Mr. Folger or any other person boarding the second compartment. I got on with my sister and shut my eyes. I wasn't sleeping but just resting all the time until the train came to a halt."

His interview with the conductor was similar to everyone else's. He did not notice anyone near the train or any cars stopped along the road. "No cars at all. No cars," he repeated. The constable did notice that the conductor, even two days later, still seemed clearly shaken up. He told the constable, "This was a very draining experience for me."

Constable Cosmo returned to his office with Deputy Donato at his side. They sat and reviewed notes. Constable started. "Okay, I think there is a missing briefcase. Definitely a missing passenger. Miguel Orozco of Sconset. Sonya, the young girl, saw him get on the train. She said he got in the same compartment as the deceased. Hmm …"

"It would be easy to disappear in the dark with all the commotion of the passengers getting off the train to view the tree," replied Donato. "So, if he's involved, who cut the tree? Couldn't be Miguel, as he was on the train."

"Maybe he's got an accomplice?"

"That's if he's even involved in the murder."

"Where's Miguel, and where's the supposed briefcase?" And what would be the motive for Miguel to murder such a gentle old man? What about the cuff link with the fabric? Whose initials are VCP?"

Constable Cosmo needed time to think and sort things out. Deputy Donato wanted to look for Miguel Orozco and get him into the station. "I'll sweat him. Sweat him good, until he cracks."

But Constable Cosmo told him, "Just to keep all this information under your belt. The town is mad with gossip. Everyone is at Les's Lunch Counter, the bar at Cy's, the Knitting Club, the Wharf Club. Every restaurant and bar is abuzz about the murder."

"I heard it's his nephew looking to get an inheritance who offed the old man," one person said.

"I heard it was an angry husband who found out his wife was getting presents from old man Folger."

And the gossip went on and on. One story that arose was it was his lawyer who had changed Folger's will and would end up getting it all.

Constable Cosmo headed down to the wharf. Every few minutes he was stopped by someone asking if he solved the case. "Who's a suspect?"

One guy even said, "When you catch 'em, let's hang him on Main Street right in public view!"

What Cosmo needed was to go to his spot—a lone bench behind the old Egan's Dry Goods store by the water. No one was ever there; it was almost like a forgotten spot. It could not be seen from the street, and you actually had to pass down a gravel alleyway to get to it. This was a place he found he could always work his mind without being disturbed.

Even in the summer months the bench stood empty like a moment, lost in time—even though he was sure, by the cigarette butts left on the ground in the summer, that some kid must have brought his girlfriend down here for some romance.

He sat on the bench in the cool weather. He could see the sun dropping off into the inlet. This time of year it started getting dark by 4:00 p.m.

Now that he was alone, undisturbed, he took out his notes. Something didn't sit right. In the back of his mind something was bothering him, but he couldn't place it. Was it something he saw? Maybe someplace at another time, but he couldn't get his mind to focus on it. What was it that kept him up for a good hour before he could fall asleep? The night prior he awoke to this thought buried in the back of his mind. What was it? He knew it would come to him, but it bothered him when issues like this compounded his thoughts.

He thought, *How could only one passenger see Miguel Orozco getting on the train?* The conductor, Jim Jaksic, always collected the fare at the end of each stop, unless the passenger had a ticket book or wanted to pay upon boarding. Constable Cosmo always thought that was a weird way to collect the fare, but some people arrived at the last minute and climbed aboard.

Cosmo sat, thinking and knowing that the Sconset Express was not like a normal train that ran from a major station to station where the conductor did not man the engines of the trains.

Now it was time to compile the facts and get the detective mode going. *Where did Miguel disappear to? Was there or was there not a briefcase with Mr. Folger on the train? And if so, where is it now, and why was he heading out to Sconset when he resided in town?*

Constable Cosmo had Deputy Donato very quietly scour the streets, train, bars, restaurants, and other local venues to see if he could spot Miguel. The deputy also hung around the bar at the Sea Cliff Hotel, trying to spot the suspect. He was nowhere to be found. He told the deputy not to ask any questions, just to see if he could locate him and, if so, not to approach him. Actually, if he did see him, he should look the other way. The deputy was confused by this but did not question the constable's methods.

As Cosmo put his thoughts in order, he again thought about the briefcase. *What was in there, and why would Miguel murder for it?*

The next day the constable was going over any leads that had come in by way of tips from people offering their ideas. He was getting ready to head out to Sconset to the Orozco home when Karen came into his office and shut the door. "Julio Orozco is in the outer office and wants to speak with you."

She went out and ushered Julio into the constable's office. He realized that they had met in the past briefly as he introduced him to Deputy Donato. Julio took a seat and told the constable that he had just heard the news about

Obadiah. He told him they had a meeting set up in Sconset on the night of the murder, but Obadiah never arrived. "I tried to call his home the next day, but there was no answer. It was late last night when a friend called me and told me about the death of Obadiah."

The person calling had no knowledge of their planned meeting, and as far as he knew, the only people who knew about the meeting were Julio, his wife, and Obadiah. Julio then explained the depth of the meeting and the fact that Obadiah was going to bring a considerable amount of cash with him for an investment.

"How much money are we talking about, Julio?"

"I'm sorry, Constable, but this is a matter of personal business. I can just say that it was quite substantial."

Constable Cosmo continued the conversation, telling Julio that the amount of cash they were discussing would not be disclosed to anyone but the three of them in the room and might only come out if there was a trial. Julio, wanting to be an upstanding citizen, told them he was carrying fifty thousand dollars that Obadiah kept in a safe-deposit box at the Nantucket Bank.

"How much?" asked the constable.

"Wow," Donato said in shock. "Why didn't he write a check?"

Julio explained, "It was Obadiah's idea, as he said he had a substantial amount of cash on hand." Julio asked if the money was with Obadiah when they discovered the body.

"No" was the answer, and they asked Julio to keep that bit of information to himself or the island would turn this into a witch hunt, so to speak.

After a few more moments, Donato asked very casually about his wife and Miguel. Julio told him that kids will be kids, and Miguel was trying to figure out his path in life. "I haven't seen Miguel since Saturday. We had a small disagreement."

After taking all this down on a notepad, they thanked Julio for stopping by and would keep him updated on their findings. Now it was starting to make sense. They had a motive and a missing Miguel, which now made him their number one and only suspect. Deputy Donato was aching to locate Miguel, bring him in, sweat him out, and close the case. He'd get his name in the paper, most likely a front-page photo. This would make him a real hero to the townsfolk.

R. H. Macy was a Nantucket boy who made his mark in retail. The balloon used for Macy's Thanksgiving Parade was designed by summer resident Tony Sarg.

CHAPTER TEN

Miguel was getting restless after he disappeared from the train. He went to Susie's Guesthouse two days. When Julio and Victoria were out of the house, he packed a bag and left a note saying he was going to stay with friends in town for a few days.

He went to the guesthouse and paid her for five days in advance. He told her he did not need any maid service, which ran an extra dollar per day, or breakfast, for that matter. Susie took the money and gave him the key to room thirteen. He could not figure out her room number system. She had only six rooms for rent, so how did she come up with a number thirteen?

He thought to himself, *Lucky thirteen—maybe it's a good omen.* He told Susie he was planning on doing some writing and needed peace and quiet. "I don't have any other rooms rented during this week, so you can have all the solitude you want. And you're by the back entryway, which no one ever uses, so you can come and go without being disturbed. Coffee is always available in the common area from 8:00 a.m. till 4:00 p.m.," she added.

Miguel dropped his bag in the room and made a short grocery list. He planned on staying in his room after the heist, lay low for a couple of days, and then take the boat to Hyannis.

Bananas, bread, sandwich meats, cheese, beer, and soda. He could put everything he needed in the refrigerator in the common area or just place them on the outer window ledge. It was cold enough outside, and no one could see it, as the window was in a back area of the house.

Constable Cosmo had gone down to the ferryboat office and asked to speak with Mr. Andresen, the captain. He asked if they could talk in private, so the captain brought him into the inner office and shut the door. "Any luck on finding your killer?" the captain asked.

"Not yet, but I'm following up on a few leads. I wanted to know if you could keep an eye out by passing through the boat prior to leaving the dock, as we discussed on the phone. I've got a better description of the person I am looking for: a man about twenty-two years old, black hair, five ten, of Spanish descent, 180 pounds, clean shaven. He will most likely be traveling alone. If you do spot him, delay the boat. Fake some engine trouble or electrical problem, and contact me. I will try to be in my office around sailing times."

"Sure thing, Constable. Do you think he's your murderer?"

"We think he might have some information about the night of the murder. Not sure, but we are checking every lead. Some people just don't want to get involved, but this would be of help if we could talk with him. Don't approach him. Just contact me. I will come right down to the ship."

Now back at his office, the constable and Deputy Donato reviewed the notes they had again. Deputy Donato, in and out of uniform, had been all over the town—at bars, restaurants, and shops—but there was no sign of Miguel.

They headed out to the Orozco home with heavy hearts. It was a quiet ride, and Cosmo felt terrible to have to break this news to Julio about Miguel being seen getting on the train at the last minute and being in the car where the murder took place. Somehow Miguel seemed to have vanished. Things of this nature just didn't happen on Nantucket.

It was 10:45 a.m. when they arrived at the estate. They knocked on the door. A nice aroma of wood burning in the fireplace filled the cool morning air. Julio greeted them with a smile. "Constable, what brings you two out here on such a fine day? Have you solved the case? Find the missing money?"

Julio quickly realized that something was very wrong. Cosmo and the deputy were not smiling and were looking over his shoulder into the house.

The constable apologized for the disturbance and asked if Miguel might be at home. Julio asked, "Why are you looking for Miguel?" Julio waved them into his study.

Cosmo explained the whole scenario as well as he knew it. "It doesn't look good, Julio, I am afraid to say. I don't know if he's involved, Julio, but even you have to admit it's odd for him to disappear like that. Looking at the facts, none of the other passengers left the scene of the crime, and he was the only one in the compartment with Obadiah."

"But Miguel would never—"

"I understand your thoughts, Julio, and we're not saying he's guilty. Still we have to do our job and follow up on all leads. Would you mind if we searched his room?"

"Yes, of course. It's right this way." Julio led them up the mahogany stair case.

Julio was still quite stunned about the meeting never taking place, the murder of his fishing partner, and now the news of Miguel. No one besides Victoria and himself knew about his meeting that was planned with Obadiah.

"Julio, dear, what's going on?" Victoria asked as she saw them coming up the stairs.

She saw the expressions on the men's faces and knew something wasn't quite right. Her first thought was that something horrible had happened to Miguel.

"Oh, no," she said, her face welling up. "What's happened? Is it Miguel?" she asked with a worried look.

Julio rushed to her side. "No, dear. I believe he's fine. They are investigating leads about the night of the murder, and Miguel was on the train."

"But he never came home that night," Victoria replied.

"Miguel left the scene. He might have been a little tipsy and not thinking clearly. Maybe he didn't want to wait around for the tree to be removed. Maybe he headed back to town. Don't worry, my love. You know how Miguel can be."

Julio relayed the story briefly to Victoria after showing the officers to Miguel's room.

Victoria was shaken at the facts laid before her by Julio, but he kept telling her, "They just need to follow up on any and all leads." Julio also was very light on giving Victoria all the facts, so as not to worry her more than she already was. "Victoria, why don't you go make us a fresh pot of coffee. When they are finished looking around, we will all join you in the kitchen."

After Victoria went down the stairs, Julio entered Miguel's room. They were just doing a general light search of his closet and desk area, not finding anything of importance. Julio talked with them, explaining that Miguel had no idea of his planned meeting, and he did not think anyone except him and Victoria had any knowledge of it. He also asked if they could tread lightly in conversation around Victoria, so as not to upset her even more, to which they readily agreed. They kept the matter on the softer side in conversation.

They all went into the kitchen, where Victoria had a plate of assorted cookies and her special honey crisps that Deputy Donato seemed to be enjoying while they went over the robbery and murder details. "Obadiah's wallet was left untouched, but they believed he was carrying a briefcase that contained the money."

"Did Miguel ever carry a knife?" asked Cosmo.

"Not that I am aware of," Julio replied. "Miguel is really a gentle soul. Sometimes a little argumentative, but not violent." Julio also mentioned that he and Miguel were not seeing completely eye to eye on his work ethics. He was now twenty-two years old and had to start acting like more of a man than a wanderer.

He explained that they wanted Miguel to go back to Santiago and help run the business with his cousin Oscar, but Miguel did not seem to have any interest. Julio also mentioned the fact that Miguel was going to have to start supporting his own lifestyle if he wasn't going to start working for a living. His last conversation a few days ago was that Miguel was going to head out on his own, possibly with Jeff Cook, to New York and work on the play sets there.

Julio felt sick to his stomach as he realized how this sounded to the constable and the deputy.

Deputy Donato just kept thinking, *This kid's spoiled. He must have committed the murder. If I could just nail him …* He could envision the article in the newspaper clear as day.

Constable Cosmo now felt even stronger about the implications of Miguel being guilty, with the possibility of Miguel being shut off from the money tree of Julio and Victoria. He kept his thoughts to himself.

They finished their coffees, told Julio to contact them if Miguel came back home, bid them farewell, and headed back to the station. He now had a corpse, a missing fifty thousand dollars, and a kid getting shut off from his cash flow.

Denis Toner walked into Cy's and sat at the bar. KW was tending to the bar and put the unpaid tab in front of him. Denis promptly pulled out a $10 bill and said, "Thanks for holding that, KW. I needed to clear up a few bills this week, and I was running a little short. But, hey, I got a raise at work this week. Can I order Sylvia's blue plate special and a glass of red wine?"

"Coming right up!" KW replied.

"Hey, KW, have you seen Miguel?" Cooker asked him while reading a script he had received in the post.

"Haven't seen him for a few days," KW said. "Maybe he's hanging out in Sconset. If I lived in that house out there, I would never leave. It's a *sweet* place!"

"He will come wandering in soon enough," KW said while placing silverware and wine in front of Denis.

"He and his dad are not getting along. Old man is gonna boot him if he doesn't straighten up and get a job!" Cooker explained, shaking his head. "Hey, KW, do me a favor and order me up the pasta with the sausages, and grab me some bread, if you don't mind."

"You want something to drink?"

"What I really want is a big old 7 and 7, but I'll stick with a soda. Gonna give my liver a break for a while … maybe a long while."

Constable Cosmo and Deputy Donato were back at the station. Something was still eating at Cosmo, but he just couldn't place it. Something was coming—he knew that for sure.

He reached down, grabbed the envelope off his desk, and pulled out the cuff link. VCP were the initials. "Who is VCP, and does it have any bearing on the case, along with the torn fabric? What does this mean?" the constable thought out loud.

For some unclear reason he felt there was something familiar about the initialed cuff link. He couldn't place it, although he knew he had seen something that resembled it before. Cosmo had shown the cuff link to Victoria and Julio. Victoria told the constable she had never seen it prior, but she felt that the torn fabric was from a shirt. "Possibly a piece of a sleeve? Miguel doesn't wear cuff links. Not his style unless it's with a tuxedo for a wedding. He is more relaxed with his dress."

Cosmo kept turning the cuff link in his fingers, thinking if he kept doing this long enough, it would come to him. He was still trying to sort out the events in chronological order. "And who cut the tree?" Cosmo called Donato into his office to bounce a couple ideas off him.

"So," he said to his deputy, pacing back and forth, "what if Miguel overhears his father talking to Obadiah about the meeting and the money? Julio wouldn't be aware of his eavesdropping. Maybe Miguel hops on the train, glad that it's just him and Obadiah in the last compartment. It's a dark night. He's planning on doing a grab-and-go. Then the next morning he takes the first boat out. Miguel would have to have an accomplice."

"He would need to," the deputy stated. "He could not get out there, cut the tree, run back to town, and hop on the train. Even though it's possible, that's eight miles back and forth. There were no tools found by the tree, but an easy throw off into the thick shrubs. It would be hard to spot anything."

"And the cuff link? VCP with an orange background and an old lady encompassed in the center—is it relevant? Was it Obadiah's? Was it a passenger's from another train ride?"

Constable Cosmo, dressed in street clothes, wandered over to Les's Lunch Counter for a cup of coffee. He asked Les if he had seen Miguel Orozco lately.

"No" was all Les replied. "Not in at least a week."

Cosmo finished his coffee and headed out. His next stops were the Ocean House and the Tap Room. Same responses there. It was getting late when he made his way over to Cy's. He spoke with KW over a bowl of minestrone soup. Again no one seemed to have come in contact with Miguel recently. Nothing was adding up to nothing. Had Miguel disguised himself and gotten on the boat? Did he hop a ride on a fishing boat?

He asked KW a few questions about the last few times he saw Miguel. He said he saw him the night of the murder at the bar. "He seemed a little jumpy, tossed back two shots of tequila and a couple beers, paid, and left."

"What time was that?"

"It was around six thirty when he came in, and he was here for about fifteen minutes."

"Did he say where he was headed when he left?"

"No, just paid and left. Didn't talk with anyone while he was here. He was alone at the last stool over there."

KW also told him that earlier in the week he was with Doug Amaral and then with Cooker a day later. "I overheard him saying he was pissed at his father, who wanted him to go work the family business in Santiago, which he had no intention of doing."

He then showed KW the cuff link and asked if he recognized it. KW said he had never seen it before. KW thought for a minute and said, "I don't know anybody with the initials VCP."

The next morning the news was all over town about Constable Cosmo calling on Julio and Victoria to inquire about Miguel. *What a small island,* he thought. Now the rumors were running rampant. No one had seen Miguel since the murder on the train, and everyone was talking about how he disappeared from the scene of the crime.

Constable Cosmo had already contacted the Cape Cod Police Barracks and the State Police Offices, as well as the Port Authority, to keep an eye out for Miguel.

Deputy Donato was at the bank to make his weekly deposit. He was deep in thought while he waited in line for the cashier to finish up with Mr. Krauter. Desperately trying to unfold his grand plan in his head, he had a gut feeling that Jeff Cook and Miguel were partners and pulled off the heist. *Starving artists. How much money can you make writing a play?* He was sure he had solved the case. He thought about how this would make him the town hero. Now all he had to do was find a way to convince the constable. He had to find a way to grab all the glory for himself. Maybe he could question Mr. Cook when the constable wasn't around. Cooker just might have some insight about where Miguel was. Once he had Miguel, the rest would unfold. *All the credit will go to me.*

Mr. Sollas was in his office when Ms. Hutton entered. "I have some good news. Mr. Toner got a raise and also a cash advance from the Ocean House. Believe it or not, he paid all the late payments on his mortgage."

"That's good to hear, June. Maybe now he won't hold any animosity towards me for not giving him the loan."

Minestrone Soup
>   1 tsp olive oil
>   1 medium onion (sweet), chopped
>   1 garlic clove, minced
>   1 cup parsley, chopped
>   3 stalks celery
>   4 carrots
>   1 potato
>   2 cans cannellini beans or kidney beans
>   2 small zucchini
>   2 qt water
>   2 qt chicken stock

Add onion and parsley to 6-quart pot. Add enough olive oil to cover bottom of pan. Cut up celery, carrots, potato, and zucchini. Sauté in pot until soft. Add garlic. Brown slightly. Put liquids in pot, and bring to a simmer for 1½ hours. Add beans, and simmer for 30 minutes.

Nantucket is a town, county, and island. From 1900 to 1918, automobiles were banned. The island is encompassed by more than eighty-two miles of beaches.

CHAPTER ELEVEN

Miguel kept his bag tucked in the closet. On his first morning, after a very restless night of pondering exactly what transpired the night prior, he departed Susie's Guesthouse for a quick stroll over to the drugstore to grab a jelly roll and a coffee. The train episode was evidently known, as he overheard two elderly ladies going on about something that happened with a downed tree blocking the train and the police being called out to the site. Miguel quickly paid for his items and retreated to his room, keeping his hat tugged down on his head and looking down. He was very grateful that it was early and he did not run into anyone he knew. Now he figured the streets were buzzing with gossip.

It was his fourth day of staying put. He was still nervous after jumping off the train. All sort of things were running through his mind. Were they searching for him? Of course they had to be. He was the only person riding with Obadiah, and he took off from the scene. If he tried to leave, someone would spot him. He had a better plan thought out, or he thought so.

Miguel walked into his parents' house late that evening. Julio's temper started to flare when he heard the door.

"Miguel! Where the hell have you been! Your mother and I have been worried sick for days."

"I know, Dad. I just needed some time to think. I'm fine. Really."

"Christ, boy. The whole police force are looking for you. What have you done?"

"What do you mean? I was at Susie's Guesthouse. No big deal, Papa."

Julio said to him, "Didn't you hear about what occurred on the train and Mr. Folger?"

"What's to hear?" Miguel replied.

"He's dead, Miguel," Julio said in a slightly somber voice.

"Dead? Dead?" Miguel repeated. "But I saw him a couple nights ago on the train."

"Yes, he was murdered the night you left the train. The whole police force is looking for you! They have interviewed everyone on the train and are seriously looking for you!"

Miguel looked confused, staring into his father's eyes as he spoke. "I was still dozing when the train stopped. I had had some tequila and beers at Cy's and had a few glasses of wine at the Ocean House prior to that, so when I awoke I was in a foggy state. I got off to see what the commotion was about. I walked past Mr. Folger. He was fine. I heard him wheezing. It sounded like he was snoring. I could see the tree was downed, so I said, 'The heck with this. I don't need the book this bad.' The only reason I was on the train was to come back to pick up a book I forgot here," Miguel continued. "I just turned and walked towards Sconset Road. I didn't want to wait around. I walked in the shadows back to the guesthouse and stayed there for the last few days."

"Well, Miguel, Mr. Folger was stabbed in the lung and died right on the train. Everyone's looking at you!"

"I swear I had no idea he had been murdered. If that was the case, I would have stopped to help."

The next morning Julio called Constable Cosmo, informing him that Miguel had returned home. "He told us that he just needed a few days to get away. To clear his mind. He says he took some clothes and stayed at Susie's Guesthouse. He says he never left the room. He slept most of the days and read a few books he brought with him. He told us he dropped off his things at the guesthouse but wanted to grab another book or two from his bedroom in Sconset. Prior to getting down to the depot, he had stopped in Cy's and had a couple of shots and beers. He got to the train right as it was leaving. He was in the backseat of the second compartment, and the only other person in it was Mr. Folger. It was quite dark out, and he was drifting off to sleep when the train came to a halt."

Constable Cosmo told Julio that he needed to get Miguel down to the station immediately so they could make heads or tails of the whole story directly from Miguel.

Julio thought it was time for him to have a stiff drink. He went into the library and poured himself a straight three fingers full of Irish whiskey into a crystal glass. He swirled the amber liquid around and thought back to Miguel's childhood—the wide sunny beaches and the nice dinners with just the three of them. They often grilled dinner on an open fire outside on the cooler nights in Santiago. He, Victoria, and Miguel were home, safe from the outside world. And now this terrible chapter was in their lives. "Miguel is mixed up in this mess, looking like a guilty man, or is he just careless in his thoughts as Miguel usually is?" Maybe this dream island was really too good to be true. But Julio knew in his heart Miguel was not a killer or murderer, no matter what situation arose.

Julio finished the whiskey and felt the warmth of it in his stomach. He went into the kitchen, where Victoria and Miguel were seated. Miguel was slowly eating a Danish, talking quietly with his mother. He looked at Julio and said, "Papa, I did nothing wrong. You have to believe me. For the last four days I have been thinking of my future. After all this mess is straightened out, I think we can come to a reasonable agreement about Santiago, Miami, and Nantucket."

That sounded like positive news to Julio. Maybe Miguel really had done some soul searching, but now they had to go face the music. "Let's go, son. Remember—your mother and I are always by your side through thick and thin. Together as a family we will stand strong."

Miguel stood, brushing the crumbs off his shirt. He hugged his mother and told her not to worry. He had done nothing wrong.

Julio and Miguel walked to the car in cold silence. The drive to town was the longest Julio had remembered. He was not in a rush to get to the station. He drove cautiously. "Not a time to hit a roaming deer."

Miguel stared straight ahead. No words. No explanations. It was agony for Julio, as Miguel was just quiet, almost in a daze.

Then it happened, right after they passed Del Winns Farm on Sconset Road. It was like a lightbulb went off in Julio's head. He knew where he had seen the cuff link. It was all a little sketchy, but he was remembering it with more and more detail as he drove toward town. He thought he had said it to himself but then realized he said it out loud, and he saw Miguel stiffen in his seat. At the same time, six miles away, Constable Cosmo had a revelation. He told his secretary, "Get down to the Atheneum. Bring me back every copy of the *Inquirer and Mirror* for the last six months."

Now did this clue that came forth in their minds have anything to do with the murder? It would all play out when Miguel's story was told.

Julio now wished he hadn't drunk the Jameson. It made his mind a little cloudy and slow. His stomach was now in a knot, and it hurt in a way it never had ached before. He knew his son was not a killer. None of this made sense. All of a sudden Julio felt years older, crumpled, and useless.

His hands on the steering wheel were sweating. They trembled as they got closer to town. He started clenching the steering wheel so tightly that his knuckles where white and his wrists began to ache.

He didn't want Miguel to see how devastating this was for him. Either way he looked at it, this was not going to be just a slap on the wrist. There was no easy fix for this situation.

When they arrived at the police station, Julio escorted Miguel, assuring him that everything would be okay. "Just tell the truth." Miguel knew what he was up against, but no one really knew the correct story, and he wasn't about to implicate himself in any way, shape, or form.

Deputy Donato took Miguel alone into the back room, where he remained silent. Donato was ready to interrogate, but the constable had told the deputy, "Just get him seated, and get him some water. I want to speak briefly with his father." Constable Cosmo came out and talked with Julio. He told him, "Maybe you should go out, get a cup of coffee, and relax."

Julio said, "No, I am going to stay by my son's side. If I feel we need counsel, I have Wesley Morris already informed, and he can be here tomorrow early morning."

The constable gave a wry smile and said, "Understood. At this point it's all just questions and answers. He's not being charged with anything. We are just trying to nail down the facts of what transpired in the compartment where the murder took place, and Miguel is our number one suspect—actually, our only suspect, but we are not saying he's guilty. Several things need to be clarified, as I am sure you can understand."

"Before we start the interview, Constable, I think I recall seeing the cuff link you showed me."

"Really?" The constable was a bit surprised and said, "That's strange. About an hour ago I thought I remembered seeing it in the past also. I sent my secretary to the Atheneum to get the last six months of the paper. In the back of my mind I thought I saw a photo of a man wearing them, but I am not completely sure of that. I think I have seen them at one point. Julio, tell me where you think you recall seeing them."

"Well, Obadiah and I had discussed meeting at the Ocean House in the front parlor room for privacy so he could explain his situation to me about wanting to invest in the precious stones business. Obadiah and I chose a couple of chairs over by the fireplace. The large wingback padded ones. When we arrived there was a group of elderly ladies off in one area, knitting. There was another couple evidently visiting, as they had travel brochures spread out on a card table. They were enjoying a pot of tea. After a while the tourists with the brochures got up to leave. The way our seats were positioned we were not facing the entry that leads through the lobby but more directly to the fireplace."

"What time was this meeting?"

"We met at 3:00 p.m., and it went on for over an hour."

"During that time did anyone come in or leave the parlor?"

"After the tourists departed, a few people came in to get a book from the library section. Another young couple that seemed as if they just checked in came and stood by the fire for a few minutes. One couple came in with the menus from the dining room and looked around for a few minutes. I explained in depth about how my grandfather had started the Orozco Fine Gems business to Obadiah and how we have been in business over seventy years in Santiago. By the end of our conversation, Obadiah was very interested. We discussed then details of our partnership, and Obadiah said he would bring the cash to Sconset. It was after that conversation that Obadiah departed. I knew the train wouldn't depart for another forty-five minutes, so I remained behind and watched the fire.

"As we stood up and shook hands, I saw the wrist of a gentleman sitting there ever so quietly, reading the newspaper in his wingback chair, almost back-to-back with me. That's when I noticed the initialed cuff links. I glanced at them quickly, not really paying attention, but the unique design caught my eye. When I went to leave, the seat behind me was empty."

The constable said, "So you think this person might have overheard your plans with Obadiah and the money?"

"I don't know," replied Julio. "I never heard the man sit down or the sound of the newspaper pages being turned. The fire was crackling away, the knitting ladies were a little loud, as they were sort of hard of hearing, a few people coming and going."

Now the constable and Julio had more to consider. Thoughts raced through Julio's mind—not the ones he wanted to think about, but he was forced to, and he was sure the constable was thinking the same thing. "Did this person overhear the investment plan, and was Miguel conspiring with this person? Oh, my, were the partners?"

Or was it just a coincidence? It seemed too distant of a connection for a man to overhear this conversation and then partner up with Miguel.

Julio racked his brain for answers, trying so hard to recall anything that made any kind of sense in this convoluted scenario.

Things were getting either better or worse in this situation. It was still foggy in his mind. A man was dead, and the money was missing. Was his son involved or not?

The constable saw that Julio was honestly struggling and overwhelmed by the situation and was relieved that Julio's wife was not with them. He put his hand on his shoulder and said, "We will be gentle. I will conduct the interview. Deputy Donato is a good man but has no experience in this line of questioning, and I felt he might jump to an early conclusion not in Miguel's favor."

"I have a feeling that my wife is wandering around the house in a fearful daze. Can I just call her quickly to reassure her before we start the interview?"

"Sure, Julio, of course." Julio made the short but uninformative call to Victoria and told her they might have made a small discovery on the cuff link connection, but it was going to be a while until they returned home.

Shortly after they went into the interview room, Deputy Donato was tapping his foot, anxious to start questioning Miguel. He knew that he could trip him up, sweat it out of him, and get the confession only if they gave him an hour alone with Miguel.

They were now all in the interview room. Miguel was asking, "Why am I here? All I did was take a train, and when it was stopped, I left."

"It's because a murder took place, Miguel," the deputy said. "And that makes you a suspect, being how you were the only one in the compartment when it took place."

The constable quieted the deputy and gently started the questioning with the morning of the murder, walking Miguel through each of his steps from when he awoke until he walked past Mr. Folger. Miguel told him how he wanted some time to think. He and his father were not seeing eye to eye on going back to Santiago. He had to get out of the house for a while. He knew it would be a bad idea to hang around town all day, as he would just end up going from bar to bar, drinking. So he booked Susie's Guesthouse the day prior.

After leaving Sconset with some books and a small amount of clothes, he planned a few days alone. He thought it might do him some good to maybe go to a movie. He didn't want to run into friends. He knew they would just drag him into the bars. He wanted to figure things out.

He left a short note in the kitchen at his house, went to town, and checked in. He went to Mignosa's Market and got some fruits, sliced meats, bread, and beer and headed back to Susie's and camped out in his room.

Later on around 5:00 p.m., he had decided he was bored, so he went to the Tap Room and sat at the end of the bar, grateful that none of his friends were in there. He had four rum and Cokes. He didn't want to go back out to Sconset to get one other book, but he thought, *Better now than tomorrow.* He knew he was more likely to run into some of his friends during the day, so he headed for the train. He stopped at Cy's around 6:45 p.m. and had two quick beers and two healthy shots of tequila. He then arrived at the train almost upon departure and climbed into the last compartment, where just an older man was seated by the front door. Miguel headed all the way to the back of the compartment, where he promptly shut his eyes and went to sleep. The next thing he knew, the train kind of jerked to a halt. He wasn't asleep, but he wasn't awake either. That was when he thought there was a slight commotion at the front of the compartment. By the time his eyes opened and focused, the only thing he recalled was that the front door was open.

Then he said, "I was still quite drunk when I walked past the old man. I thought he was dozing. I saw the tree downed and figured, screw this, I don't need the book that bad, and I walked back to town. I went directly to Susie's and passed out in bed." He said he never left the guesthouse until he decided to just go back home to his own room. "I realized I had been drinking a lot more in the last few months, and I didn't like what I saw in the mirror or the relationship with my parents lately. We've always been such a close-knit family. That's when I realized the alcohol was fueling most of my problems. I only bought a pack of six beers for the whole four-day period, and they were gone shortly after the first day. My mind started to feel clearer than it had been in a while. I actually began to feel better, more healthy, except the sandwiches, chips, and candy bars weren't the best choice for my appetite."

Deputy Donato was chomping at the bit to get into the questioning, but every time he started the constable gave him a pretty stern look and said, "Let's just go with the flow I have established."

The deputy frowned but obeyed, thinking over and over, *I could crack this case wide open in no time!*

When the last of the questions were finished and Deputy Donato had compiled all his notes on the interview, he started in: "Now there's a few things I would like to clarify."

As he was turning the pages of the notes, the constable quickly said, "That's enough for today, Deputy. You may go."

They left Miguel in the interview room alone while the constable and Julio had a discussion about the interview. He said, "You're free to go, but make sure it's clear to Miguel that he's not to leave the island."

Right then the station door opened, and in walked Karen McRedmond. She was carrying a few paper bags full of newspapers. "Twenty-six of them. One for each week in the last six months."

"Splendid, Karen, just splendid," said the constable. "Now this shouldn't take long if the three of us can each take a stack of papers. We can spread them out on the conference table."

"But what are we looking for?" asked Julio. Karen also had a bewildered look on her face.

"Turn every page, one by one. We are looking for an article that might have a photograph of the mysterious cuff links."

After about five minutes of carefully scanning the pages, Karen very excitedly shouted out, "I found it! Look here."

Right in the top center was a shot of a man holding a gift box with the exact cuff links. The caption under the photograph read, "Denis Toner of Nantucket Island wins the Veuve Clicquot top salesperson award for New England." Bob Rubin, of Ruby Wines, was handing Mr. Toner a boxed set of VCP Grande Dame cuff links and a check for two hundred dollars.

Julio looked excitedly at the constable. "Do you know this person?"

"Yes. I do in a way. I'm on the board of the Nantucket Bank, and Mr. Toner was just recently denied a loan with us. Until yesterday he was a few months behind on his mortgage at Pacific National Bank. I got a memo from Mr. Sollas and Ms. Hutton stating that his mortgage is now in good standing. Mr. Toner brought in a check yesterday and paid up to date.

"Now this all seems to tie in. His debts were piling up. He works at the Ocean House. Lunch is over around two thirty in the afternoon. Maybe on his break he goes into the front parlor of the hotel where you and Obadiah were meeting, overhears the conversation, and puts it all together. He cuts the tree down after the train comes in from Sconset and waits in the woods. The train stops, he opens the door in the commotion, grabs the briefcase from Mr. Folger. Maybe Obadiah put up a slight struggle, so Toner pulled out his knife and stabs him and escapes before Miguel comes to his senses. Obadiah is lightly gasping, and it sounds like he's snoring. Miguel pays no attention and gets off the train."

Julio and the constable go back into the interview room. He tells Julio not to act surprised or make any comment, just to stand there quietly and watch Miguel's reaction to what the constable says. "Okay," Julio said, "let's go in."

Upon entering, Miguel said, "Can I go now?"

"In a moment," the constable replied. "Just a few more questions. Do you think or remember at all if there was a struggle with Mr. Folger? Did you see anyone enter the compartment?"

"No, but I thought I heard someone or something, but then again I was dozing off. The only thing I remember, which was odd, was that the door was already opened. It must have been from the outside, as Mr. Folger was sleeping.

165

Or so I thought. When I got off, a few people were in front of the train. Not a soul near our compartment."

"Do you know a Denis Toner?"

"I don't think so, but if he's ever in the bars I might have seen him, but no, I don't know who he is personally."

"Okay, Miguel. You are free to go. Don't discuss any of this interview with anyone else except your mother and father. This is an ongoing investigation, and we should hopefully have it wrapped up soon. Thank you for your time and cooperation in this delicate matter."

Miguel walked in silence as a free man for now, but who knew? It seemed he could still be a suspect in the murder. Julio would tell him the latest development when they were in the privacy of the car.

As Julio and Miguel walked toward the car, a black-and-white cat crossed in front, looked at Miguel, and let out a loud meow.

Miguel laughed and said, "Hello, Marshmallow."

Julio looked at him and said, "You know the cat's name?"

"Sure do. She's the house cat at Cy's Green Coffee Pot."

A few minutes after Julio and Miguel left the station, Constable Cosmo called the bank and spoke with Mr. Zises. He asked him if he could look into Mr. Toner's deposit history for the last five days.

"I can have that information shortly. I will ring you back within thirty minutes."

Constable Cosmo went to Deputy Donato's desk and told him they were heading out soon. The deputy asked, "Where to?"

The constable told him, "I think I might have solved the case."

"Did Miguel confess when you went back in the interview room?"

"Not quite, but I will explain it to you on the drive."

Twenty minutes later Mr. Zises was on the phone with the constable. He had gathered the information he requested. "Would you like a typed letter describing the latest transactions?"

"Well, yes, but first give it to me verbally. I will write it down, and I will need a typed copy if it's what I think it will show. What did you discover?"

"Well, it looks like he had a balance of $18.39 for the last few weeks. Then three days ago he made two deposits on the same day—one at the Main Street branch for $400 and one at the Pleasant Street branch for 200. Then again the following day he made two more deposits. At the Pleasant Street branch he deposited another $300. Later that afternoon he made yet another deposit at the Main Street branch for 200. These were all made in cash. Then nothing since. He did come in with a check for his mortgage two days ago, which totaled $230 for the past-due months, and his next current payment is not due until the twenty-third of this month."

Cosmo thanked Mr. Zises and asked if they could get a typed-out summary on his desk as soon as possible and hung up. He and Deputy Donato got in the squad car and headed toward Mr. Toner's residence on Back Street. He filled the deputy in on the latest development. Donato kept thinking, *There goes my case and my hero's story!* But in his last-ditch effort, he thought maybe Mr. Toner and Miguel were connected. Mr. Toner could have cut the tree. Miguel could have been a lookout or distraction on the train if needed.

They parked down the street and walked up for a slight element of surprise instead of parking directly out front. Just as they were about to knock on the front door, it opened, and

Mr. Toner, who seemed a little discombobulated, grabbing for a piece of luggage, was there. His glasses were slightly crooked, and a scarf was tossed around his neck. He did not even notice the officers directly out in front of the glass storm door.

When he noticed them, the blood drained from his face. His expression turned blank. "Going somewhere, Mr. Toner?" asked the constable as they swung open the storm door.

Denis resigned himself to the moment and set his bag back down but kept the satchel over his shoulder. The constable explained that they were following up leads on the murder of Obadiah Folger and asked if they might step inside. Denis, at a loss for words, started to babble, saying he was late for the boat and going off island to look after his aunt who had Parkinson's disease.

"Oh, this won't take but a minute," reassured the constable.

They escorted Denis to the dining room table and told him to have a seat. Deputy Donato headed to the bedroom and came out with a shirt. "Constable, I found this in a pile of laundry on the floor." The shirt was torn near the cuff. It was the same material as the one they found on the train. A few minutes later he appeared with the matching cuff link.

The deputy gave both items to the constable. He placed them on the table in front of Denis. He said, "Where's the other cuff link, Mr. Toner?"

Denis just sat with an expressionless face and said, "I think I would like to speak with my lawyer, Aul Kokelvech, if you don't mind."

"One more thing, Mr. Toner," the constable said. "Would you please open your satchel?"

"I don't want to touch it, just want to look inside," Constable stated.

Neatly packed inside was an envelope with two thousand dollars. The constable had a feeling that upon a little more digging he would reveal the rest of the money inside the suitcase.

He also told Denis, "We know that you were in the parlor of the Ocean House the afternoon that Mr. Orozco and Mr. Folger had discussed the delivery of fifty thousand dollars to Mr. Orozco by Mr. Folger. We found a piece of fabric we are certain will match up to this shirt here, and we also discovered the other cuff link. The match to this one we found at the scene of the crime."

Deputy Donato added, "Do you know a Miguel Orozco?"

Denis looked at him and replied, "I want to speak to my attorney."

They cuffed Mr. Toner and gathered the evidence. One thing they also collected was an ice pick in the kitchen dish draining area. Upon a closer look at the puncture wound, the doctor who examined Mr. Folger said it was more like a puncture than a knife wound.

They drove back to the station with Mr. Toner safely ensconced in the backseat. Once they had Mr. Toner in a cell, the constable called all the departments he had contacted earlier during this investigation, letting each one of them know the latest developments.

Mr. Toner's attorney arrived a short time later, and the next line of questioning started. The constable explained that if Mr. Toner cooperated, things would go much more smoothly all around. After discussing things in private with his attorney, Aul, Mr. Toner came forth with almost the whole truth. When asked if he had an accomplice, he flatly said, "No!"

He said he had walked out to the four-mile marker earlier on and waited until the 6:00 p.m. train passed, heading into town. He cut the tree and waited. The minute the train stopped, he spotted Mr. Folger in the second compartment. It was dark, but he knew Mr. Folger's tall height would make him stand out. Mr. Toner wore all black with a ski mask over his face. He noticed that there was only one other person in the second compartment who was not stirring when the train stopped. Denis opened the door quickly and went to grab the briefcase. Mr. Folger started to resist, so he plunged the ice pick into his body. Immediately he went limp. Right as he was exiting the train, the person at the rear of the compartment started to move. By then Denis was gone and was walking toward town, where he had his car backed into the woods near the three-mile marker, unseen from the road.

The constable collected all the money and counted it. Counting the eleven hundred in deposits, the two thousand he found in the satchel, and the money found in three manila envelopes inside the suitcase, they were short twenty grand.

Mr. Toner said he had nothing more to offer. As they led him to his cell, he mumbled to himself, "What have I done?"

Constable Cosmo contacted Bob Rubin a few days later, asking a question that bothered him. "What exactly did VCP stand for on the cuff links?"

"It stands for the widow Madame Veuve Clicquot Ponsardin—or the Grande Dame, as she was referred to after her husband passed away. Many were doubtful, back in the latter part of the 1700s, whether she could keep the champagne house afloat. She turned out to be one tough lady and gained the name of the Grande Dame of champagne."

With that understood, Cosmo said to himself, "Even long deceased, the widow Clicquot helped solve the case."

At the very moment of Denis's arrest, Neil Krauter was opening a bottle of Veuve Clicquot and pouring two glasses, which had strawberries in the bases of the flutes, for him and yet another beautiful woman who was wearing nothing but a bearskin rug and a smile. She was sitting in front of his mammoth roaring fireplace overlooking the beach at Eel Point.

The rest of the money was never recovered. Lots of island gossip was going around. The police kept an eye out for new boats or cars that did not fit into one's financial profile but to no avail.

Cooker went on, a while later, to write a screenplay that was directed by his good friend John Shea: *Life on an Island*. It debuted at the Sconset Casino and ran on Broadway for eighty-two consecutive shows. At the very first showing on Broadway, seated dead center in the first row was none other than Hunter Laroche.

Somewhere, someplace, someone had the money, but that was a different story for a different day.

Constable Cosmo told Deputy Donato and Karen McRedmond to meet him at 7:00 p.m. at Cy's. Dinner was on him, and it was time to visit with Marshmallow and enjoy some of Ms. Sylvia's fine home cooking.

After enjoying a fabulous evening and a wonderful meal, Karen left Constable Cosmo and Deputy Donato at Cy's. As she passed the Dreamland Theater, she couldn't help but notice the announcements for the upcoming shows: "*Spellbound*, the Alfred Hitchcock movie starring Ingrid Bergman and Gregory Peck opening on Thursday. All movies 35 cents."

The program on the front window showed the next film to be the Agatha Christie movie *And Then There Were None*, about a group of ten guests who are invited to an isolated island for the weekend by a mystery host, only to be killed off one by one. Could one of them be the actual killer? As she looked away from the sign, she bumped into Hunter Laroche.

CPSIA information can be obtained
at www.ICGtesting.com
Printed in the USA
FFOW05n1409061015

9 781504 918787